The Cretorian Knight's Ring

J.C. Rose

The Cretorian Knight's Ring

The Cretorian Knight Archives

The Cretorian Knight's Ring is a work of fiction. Names, characters, places, and incidents are the product of the author's imagination or are used fictitiously. Any resemblance to actual persons, living or dead, events, or locales is entirely coincidental.

ISBN: 979-8-9939881-1-5

First paperback edition April 2026

Book Cover Illustration by Ertac Altinoz

Map of the Midlands

DEDICATION

For those who carry a deep wound… may you heal and your heart not yield…

CHAPTER 1: PEACE OR...

A man is an eternal slave of loyalty. He either abides by it or must live chained in the shadows of betrayal.

"Is that what I believe it to be?" Darius asked as the coins and rings crashed on the table. Lionus, without hesitation, knew that which he mentioned.

The pair were in a lone inn within Broondwood, not far off from Accreton. They had come here to rest after their travels. Within, some men sang and roared, while others murmured about quests and secrets.

Lionus reached for the silver ring. *It is truly mesmerizing. The craftsmanship is impeccable.* It had a dragon head, its eyes glowing, as if its ruby gems withheld the flame of its dragon bond. The entire ring appeared to be made of dragon scales, craftsmanship merely heard through the tales of bards, a piece to never be held by the common man. Founded in the Era of Ashes, Lady Isabel's time, and reshaped by one woman. One woman who few would imagine could grasp such power, let alone hold it. Lady Isabel of House Valenour had come to reshape the land after a family secret was bestowed upon her years ago. For a woman to hold such power in their land was an unbelievable feat. If Isabel had been a noblewoman who altered history, the woman who reshaped the rings had proven to be as resourceful as Isabel herself.

Lionus' breathing stalled as he stared at the ring. He leaned into it, as if it was calling out to him with its splendor. He smiled while he was looking at it, then he glanced at Darius. "Are you seeing what I am seeing?"

"It cannot be. A Cretorian Knight's ring," Darius snatched it from Lionus' hand. He gazed within, his emerald eyes admiring the inscriptions. Removing his gauntlet, he was about to put it on...

Lionus seized his wrist. "Do not."

Darius' head snapped toward him. "Why not?", his eyes wide.

Lionus studied his friend. The pair were mercenaries, and their last quest had brought them down towards the region of Ashencrest, home of the Valenours in Accreton. They could be mistaken for brothers, for both bore the obsidian hair from the island of Emeros, their bronze skin now lighter that they had moved south. He shifted his gaze towards the ring.

"To wear the ring is to be marked by it," Lionus pointed at the band where there was a minute hole. *If it stabs you, will it cut through your finger and remain fixed onto the bone? It cannot. That cannot be.* Lionus shuddered at the thought.

"Do you believe I will be bothered by a prick on my finger when I acquire all its strength?"

Why does he believe it is his to keep? Why does he believe he will be the one who becomes a dragonrider?

"Strength, or do you simply mean for it to aid in your ambitious ways?" a woman's voice came from behind Lionus.

The pair turned, Lionus glancing over his shoulder at the woman who appeared. She was of lengthy, wavy, blond hair, and unlike the pair, she had maintained the bronze color of her skin from the isles. She gazed at them, her jade eyes narrowed. There was a pause.

Lionus sighed. *You really are going to get him started.*

Her serious semblance escaped her, and a playful grin overcame her. "Do not get riled up, Darius, it is merely a jest."

"Lionus," Darius frowned, "you should lecture your woman on dealing with men."

"Eleni," Lionus glanced back at her while shaking his head. He bit his lip as he held in a chuckle. *She will not let this one escape her.*

Eleni's eyebrows rose, and she crouched behind Lionus, her thin fingers resting on his shoulder while she peered from behind him at Darius. "Shield me, husband. How will I ever protect myself from Darius the Damnable?"

Lionus could not hold back, a chuckle escaping him. He reached for her hand on his shoulder, her skin soft, like a lady of the realm.

Darius' narrowed his eyes at her, but Eleni merely laughed.

Eleni rose and wrapped her arms around Lionus. He faced her, the flowery scent rising between them as her soft cheek brushed his stubbled chin. She reeled away slightly, then leaned back in. Staring momentarily into her jade eyes, he reached for her neck and pulled her in gently, planting a kiss on her lips.

Darius rolled his eyes and grabbed his mug. Just as he began sipping, a man crashed against him. The ale fell upon his chainmail, and Darius jolted. The ring slipped from his grip, striking the table with a sharp clink before rolling across its surface. Lionus smacked his hand upon it, trapping it as the mercenary turned towards Darius.

"Watch it, bandit," Darius slammed the mug on the table.

"Who are you calling a bandit?" the mercenary asked in a low tone as he lowered himself, his face inches from Darius'.

"I assumed you would be a clever fellow. Seems I was mistaken," Darius closed the gap between them and sneered.

Lionus tucked the ring away. He glared at the bandit, the bandit's gaze darting between him and Darius. The hairs on the back of his neck rose. *Darius, let him be. We do not need any more trouble. Our last quest gave us enough of it.*

"Let me be, it is all I have," a man from the table across from them said as a pair of mercenaries surrounded him.

One of them sat him down, holding his shoulders while a man in plate armor sat across. "A debt is a debt. We said we would come to collect our protection coin," the plated mercenary said.

Eleni pulled a chair and sat beside Lionus, the trio glancing at the commotion occurring ahead. Her hand slid under the table and across his thigh. He reached for it, and her hand was clammy, a sensation he rarely felt from her. She glanced at him, the playful look which once overtook her now gone. She blinked rapidly, her hand tense as he kept his hand over hers. He furrowed his eyebrows. *You are fearless woman. What is the matter?* Before he could whisper it, there was a slap.

Their attention returned once more to the man ahead.

Lionus said across the table, "Let the man be."

"Or what?" a man behind him said. A monumental shadow cast over him, as if an eclipse overcame the sun, or in this moment, as if a blanket doused the flames in the inn.

"Here I thought we would avoid trouble. This does not concern us," Darius rolled his eyes.

"A knight must protect the weak and commonfolk," Lionus added, clutching his mug and taking a sip, his muscles tightening.

"Ah, you are a knight," the mercenary behind Lionus mumbled, letting out a laugh.

"In truth, he is not, though he would gladly claim the title." Darius shook his head. "We are travelers."

We are not travelers. Mercenaries would be the correct term at its best. Darius truly wishes to avoid this fight. But can we? Can we truly allow these men to harass the people in this inn freely?

"A knight is a code, not a title," Lionus said, then took a second sip.

"Well, Sir knight, will you pay the man's debt?" the mercenary added, chuckling. He placed his hand on Lionus' pauldron.

Darius looked up at the mercenary, clicking his tongue.

Without looking at the mercenary, Lionus glanced at Darius. There was a slight smile on his lips, as if he was intrigued by the setting unraveling around them.

Just as Lionus was about to set his mug down, the mercenary snatched it from him. Lionus, however, remained unmoved. He wrinkled his nose. *Oh, a grievous error. Never touch a man's belongings.*

There was a gurgling sound, followed by a spit. The mercenary slid it into Lionus' palm. "Take a sip, and we might reconsider the debt," the mercenary said.

We must remain calm. Lionus remained silent. He closed his eyes momentarily. *To do, or not to do. Ah, peace is our ally. They really want to fight us today. We will not. No, we will help the man. But as Darius said, we do not need any trouble.* "Judging by your smell, I would have to say my ale is ruined," Lionus added as he looked up at him.

"Ha, a jester," the mercenary laughed, his men laughing in harmony.

The remainder of the crowd in the inn remained silent, and the innkeeper had come to a halt serving ale. He shook his head in disapproval, sighing.

"I have a jest for you, my friend," the mercenary said, then moved to the side.

With the back of his fingers, he stroked Eleni's cheek, sliding his finger down her neck. "Is this why you keep this pretty woman with her flowery scent? To mask the musky smell of us han'some folk?"

Eleni clutched Lionus' thigh tighter. Her eyes widened. Lionus ground his teeth, his body tense. *Touch my wife, and that's the last time your hand will be attached to your wrist. He will fear me more than any man fears Malefic.* He squeezed her hand.

"The nice knight," the mercenary added, glancing at Lionus. "I have heard of knights such as you. They say nice knights never fight. I suppose you never fight, then. If knighthood is a code and not merely a title, then you are no a true knight, and any title or code you bear is meaningless."

Darius replied, "Title or code, he is remembered as the kind knight." He released his mug. A second mercenary placed a hand on his pauldron, and Darius frowned.

"It is but one and the same," a third mercenary beside Eleni said, reaching for her blonde braid.

Eleni yanked her braid, then cast a steely glare upon him.

Darius clicked his tongue, then replied, "As I said earlier, you lads are not the sharpest dagger in the smithy's shop. There is a very thin line between being nice and kind."

"And what is that?" the mercenary turned to Darius as he clutched his sword's pommel.

Lionus' heart thundered at the rate of a thousand war drums. His chest was about to tear. With each moment that passed with Eleni clutching his thigh, he felt the world's pillars weakening, as if it all would come crushing around them. There was nothing he hated more in this world than someone touching his wife, and that line had been stepped on and crossed.

"It is but one and the same," Darius said, smirking at Lionus. "Peace?"

Lionus inhaled, his shoulders rising as he caught his breath, his heart's pounding coming to a sudden halt.

"No." He squeezed Eleni's clammy hand, then reached for his hidden dagger. Lionus furrowed his eyebrows, and he met Darius' gaze. "Not peace. Pieces."

CHAPTER 2: THE CRETORIAN RING

It was not long before the mercenaries were dust in the wind, not one soul left alive. After the fight, they were banished from the inn. Though they emerged victorious and saved the poor lad from his debtors, they had lost their lodging for the night. The innkeeper initially appeared glad that they eliminated the inn's tormentors, but upon noticing the wrecked state his inn was in, he had banned them indefinitely.

"Where to now?" Darius asked as he rode his horse, leading the group.

"To Accreton. We have a quest to fulfill. We can rest when we are dead," Lionus said. Darius nodded, and they continued their trek through the cover of night.

Lionus wrapped his arm around Eleni as they rode together. During the skirmish, one of the mercenaries had stolen her horse, forcing them to share a mount. Though it proved no hindrance, Lionus preferred it.

"It has been quite some time since we rode together," Lionus murmured against her ear while holding the reins around her.

A smile graced her lips as she looked at him. With her before him, there was a lightness in his limbs he could not begin to explain, as though the weight of the world had been lifted from his body.

"We always ride together," she rested her head against his shoulder.

"Not like this. We have not ridden on horseback together for many moons now. I longed for it," he leaned into her, her lips brushing against his cheek.

"Am I seeing Lionus' gentler side now?" Eleni pursed her lips.

"For you, my dear, there is nothing more than my soft side." And he did not lie. *I could never be hard on her. Ever since the day I met her, she stole my heart. Those blonde locks, that gentle smile, that caring side, and that ruthless warrior. Even as a ruthless warrior, she has always been mine to protect.*

She looked at him with such a softness in her eyes that it robbed him of any thought of roughness. Even on their cloudy days, he could not help but be gentle with her. There was no armor against this woman. The lengths he would go to guard her knew no bounds. There was nothing he would not do if it meant she would live another day, be it with him or without him.

"And it is because of this that you have stolen my heart," Eleni smiled, then reached for his cheek. "I love you, Lionus. More than you can imagine."

"I know. As do I. I would spare nothing to keep you safe. You are the finest family I could ever hope to have," Lionus held both reins with his right hand so he could wrap his free arm around her.

Eleni's cheeks ripened at his regard, and she turned away. She glanced down, as though he had stirred a tempest in her belly.

"What troubles you?" Lionus cocked an eyebrow.

"It is nothing. I am merely tired," she said, her body stiffening against his.

Lionus tugged her closer and squeezed her gently, Eleni's body relaxing momentarily. "What troubles you, Eleni? You have been frightened since the inn. You have not been yourself."

"I am well. Nothing troubles me. I simply require rest," she said, pressing her fingers upon her lips. Eleni glanced around the forest, then dug her fingers into the horse's mane, as if seeking comfort within it.

"As do I," Darius stated from ahead. "The lot of you blabbering is making me ill."

"I believe it was that spit ale you drank before we got banished from the inn," Lionus laughed.

"Had I drunk the one with the spit, it would have served me far better than the one I took from you," he said without turning.

Do not remind me. I was not even able to finish my drink.

"Let us rest," Darius said as he brought his horse to a halt. "This seems like a suitable place to camp."

They came to a halt in Dryadon's Pass, one of the valleys leading towards Accreton. It was not long before they tied their horses, built a campfire, and rested amongst it.

That night, Lionus was nestled alongside Eleni. She shifted relentlessly. Unable to sleep, he opened his eyes and met her steady gaze. *What is troubling you? Why will you not tell me?* He slid his hand around her waist and pulled her closer. She smiled sheepishly, reaching for his face, circling her thumb along his jaw.

"You cannot sit still tonight," Lionus whispered while tucking a strand of hair behind her ear. "What bothers you, Eleni?"

She pursed her lips and let her eyes close for a brief moment. When she opened them again, she sought his. "Lionus, I am well."

It certainly does not seem like so. Is she hiding what troubles her? Has she fallen ill? Is she injured from the battle? "Tell me, what ails you?" His stomach clenched when she did not reply, and his heartbeat accelerated.

"Nothing. I am beyond well," she let out a smile. "I cannot be happier. For a moment… in that inn, I was frightened."

"Why?" *Eleni is never frightened. There is certainly something amiss.*

She paused.

Woman, you kill me with your silences.

"I did not wish to lose you. I cannot lose you."

"And you will not. I will remain by your side. The world will never set us apart. I swear it. I will always defend my kin," his heart pounded with every word, as if it too knew it must fight for their safety.

"I know you will not," she said, "you have always proven it to be true. I merely hope the burden will not increase when it is two."

"You mean Darius?" he replied while cocking an eyebrow.

Eleni simply chuckled. "Darius is a grown lad. He can care for himself," she glanced down.

It was then that he finally understood. *It cannot be. Can it be? Is it true?* "Am I-. Will I?" His eyes widened. *Will I truly be a father?*

Eleni bit her lip and nodded. She took his hand in hers and brought it over her belly.

His heart leapt. It came alive once more, pounding as it had in the inn hours earlier. "I will be a father?" *I always knew we would have a family. Yet, so soon? A family with Eleni… It cannot be. I cannot believe this is truly happening.* Lionus stared at her incredulously.

"Aye," she smiled.

He could not help but bring her closer to him. He kissed her forehead gently, raking his fingers through her hair as he brought her head against his chest. The fire behind them crackled lightly, and his chest felt fuller with the idea of Eleni and him starting their own family. *It cannot be. I will be a father. Eleni and I will have our family. The gods have blessed us. But in this world? How will I protect both? Am I ready? I am. They are my kin. The idea of them being hurt... No. I will not allow it. But how will I protect them if we are on the road?*

"Be still, your heart," she said as she pushed away from his chest, resting her hand upon it. As if her touch was a magic elixir, his heart eased. He stared into those jade eyes, those jade eyes he could not imagine a life without. *What would I do without you, Eleni?*

"I will do all in my power to protect you, Eleni. Trust this."

"I know you will, as you have always done."

Then, he remembered. He knew how he would secure a home for them all. The ring must be returned to the Valenours in Accreton, the last known family of dragonriders in Emerion. He was certain they would be rewarded handsomely for it, particularly amidst the Valenours' civil war. It was in his care. The group had agreed he should carry it after the battle at the inn. Once returned, they would all share in the generous coin he was certain they would receive.

He clutched his chest, pulling the ring from his necklace, "When we return this to the Valenours, we will have the riches to build our new home. Peace will wait for us, for our little boy to grow."

"Perhaps girl," Eleni said. There was this certainty in her eyes, and he could not help but imagine it to be true.

Lionus grinned. "A strong girl, like her mother. Aye."

Eleni chuckled, "And strong-hearted like her father."

"Ahhh," leaves rustled and crashed as a figure dropped from the tree above. A hooded figure landed beside them. "As much as I detest ruining family dreams, it seems you carry something I require. A pretty little trinket."

Darius leapt, and swiftly after, there was a whistle. The hooded figure's hood fell, revealing his pointed ears and pale eyes. Lionus and Eleni sprang up, Lionus standing before her while pushing Eleni behind him to shield her.

"My next arrow will not miss," Darius said, aiming at the elf.

"You reckless humans," the elf said as a streak of blood rushed down his temple. "My archers have you surrounded. There is nothing you can do to spare your lives." He raised his hand, and three arrows whistled by. They struck the bark of the tree beside them.

Eleni closed in on Lionus as he held her hand. With his other hand, he unsheathed his throwing knife, his knuckles white as he gripped it.

"One dagger cannot save you," the elf said. As he spoke, Darius closed in on Lionus, bow aimed at the elf. "Do you truly believe the three of you can destroy my clan?"

Lionus stepped back, tugging Eleni closer to him. Lionus was at a loss for words, his own hands clammy. It was not the fire of losing life itself, but of failing his promise. *I will protect you. I swear it.* But then there was a tug. Then a scream. He attempted to grip Eleni's hand, but the figure's sudden pull tore her from his grasp.

Lionus spun, and before him stood a sight he never believed he would behold–an elf holding Eleni, a dagger pressed to her throat. Sweat beaded Lionus' brow as he unsheathed his sword.

"Unhand me!" Eleni screamed.

"Release her, or I will end you all!" Lionus' temples throbbed at the sight of his enemy.

"You will all die before you take a step towards us," the elf said. "Hand over the ring."

In the distance, farther than where the other elves stood, Lionus spotted a shimmer–a group of knights had begun to approach. Though distant, he could see their crested helmets and ruby capes under the moonlight. *Cretorian Guards... Why are they here? Do they seek to reclaim the ring as well?* The knights, however, remained silent, hiding amongst the brush. The elves, though of keen senses, must have missed them amidst their discussion.

"Just hand them the ring, Lionus," Darius added, "they will slay us. We cannot survive this."

Darius is not mistaken. We will not survive. They will slay us all. The mere thought of it caused his arms to tighten, his thighs to tense. The knights continued to approach. *Wait... Darius is not mistaken? Darius never yields. Why does he yield now?*

"Hand them over, Lionus," Darius said. As Lionus pivoted, he saw the knights ever closer. Lionus grimaced. There was no sense in what was unfolding. Nevertheless, he knew they could fight their way free. That was, if there existed the slim chance that the knights joined the battle against the elves before they were annihilated. *Something is amiss. Did Darius spot the knights as well? Perhaps they are on our side.*

"You are not mistaken, Darius. We *are* defeated." Lionus faced the elf and stabbed the point of his sword into the ground. He removed the ring from his necklace. *This will lure him in while the knights approach.* He stretched his hand towards the elf. The elf tilted his head, then smiled.

"Wise human," he said as he took it.

Around them, there was silence. Then, a couple of elves disappeared, the Cretorians eliminating them with ease. As the elf before him took the ring, Lionus was certain those were his last words. Lionus smiled cockily. Before the elf pulled away, Lionus snatched his hand. As he drove him to the ground, he flung his dagger at the neck of the elf holding Eleni. Lionus unsheathed a second dagger and struck the neck of the elf who took the ring. There was a gurgling sound, the elf's eyes widening. In the silence of his death, the screams of chaos erupted all around.

Darius roared, and Lionus clutched the elf's neck as the battle began. He looked him in the eye, the pale eyes losing what little life they had. "Never threaten my family."

Lionus wrenched his dagger free, blood spattering from the elf's neck, then rose and fought off the charging elves. Eleni and Darius battled the incoming men and pointy ears, Lionus uncertain of their future. An elf rushed towards him, and Lionus threw his dagger, striking him right on his chest. The elf stopped in his tracks, falling on his knees and plopping lifeless on the ground. *We are outnumbered.*

As he turned, Eleni stood before him. She shot an arrow at an incoming elf, and he hit the ground. She then spun, ducked, slashed her sword at another's knee, and as he crashed on the grass, she twirled her sword and struck his chest.

Ruthless woman. It is not over until we all fall.

The Cretorian Guards met the elves, and he knew that perhaps they were not safe, but at least there was a chance to flee. Lionus cared little for battle now. All that mattered was the safety of his family. Amidst the roars, he turned, his gaze searching for Eleni's.

Their gazes met, and she quickly rushed towards him.

He froze. Behind her, an elf released an arrow. Lionus' fingers became cold, and a chill ran down his spine, slow and deliberate.

The closer she got, the more his stomach tightened.

This cannot be happening.

She was still rushing towards him, closing the distance. With each step, his stomach grew tighter, like a snake coiling around itself. Lionus lunged forward, reaching for her, then turned to shield her with his body…

Eleni whimpered.

The arrow pierced her back and tore through her, the force shuddering into him as its edge scraped the links on his chainmail at his belly. Her chin hit his shoulder, Eleni gasping as her body sagged against his.

A second arrow was released, and he turned her, this time, the arrow striking his own back. Lionus gasped as a tearing pain penetrated his back. Eleni fell as his body weakened, but Lionus did not release her.

Another arrow struck his back. What little strength remained within him dissipated. Lionus gasped, hoping to regain the air he lost. The taste of iron made him shiver, the thought of death ever so near.

They fell side by side, staring into each other's eyes. There was a wheeze from Eleni, and she reached for her belly.

"Our child."

"No, no," Lionus said.

He could barely breathe, every pant painful. There was a heaviness in his chest, like a horse lying on top of him. He could not choose between speaking or breathing, but in those moments, he could care little for his own air.

"Stay, Eleni. Stay… with… me…" he reached for her belly, then her face.

She reached for his own cheek, the warmth of her blood staining his face. "You never failed me, Lionus, remember that."

"I… did…" he said between breaths. He reached for his back, feeling the arrow's shaft. In one move, he snapped the shaft and groaned. Pain shot down his back, and he repeated it with the second arrow. "Ahh!"

"Gentle breaths," she repeated as she paled. *I cannot lose you.*

Lionus trembled, his limbs weakening. Eleni kept repeating herself, then placed her other hand on his chest. He did not regain his strength, but her calming tone eased his breathing. Even with an arrow in her belly, her health seemed to be deteriorating while Lionus' pain from his injuries diminished. *Why is she worsening quicker than me? A wound to the belly is a slow death.*

"You fought for us 'til the end. For me. For our family," she said, her touch becoming cold on his cheek.

Lionus inched closer, "Do not go… stay with me."

Eleni took his hand, and though it was cold, there was a colder object upon it, a dragon ring on her finger he had never seen.

"Lionus," she snatched his attention. She looked deep into his eyes, the jade in her eyes diminishing as she weakened with every passing moment. There was a gash on her leg, blood gushing through her leather armor.

Eleni cannot die. Our child cannot die. I cannot lose them both. Neither of them. Lionus pressed her wound and Eleni tugged him closer.

"Lionus, I beg you, come closer," she said, bringing him closer as he continued pressing his hand to her thigh, her warmth escaping into his palm.

I cannot let her die. I cannot let them die. My family. My child. My wife. My love.

"Please, Lionus. It is cold," Eleni whimpered, her chin trembling. As if her coldness hit him, he too began to tremble again, a chill running down his spine as her bronze skin paled swiftly.

"Stay with me, Eleni. Please. I beg you."

"Just hold me… Hold me one last time… like our horse rides. Like the last time. Like the first time. I do not wish to leave so cold."

Her words tore at his chest, beyond the immeasurable pain elicited by the arrows, arrows that seemed insignificant now.

"I am here, my love. I am here," he kept his gaze on her, his stomach quivering as her life slipped away.

Eleni smiled, a tear rolling down her cheek, "I love you, Lionus. Promise you will always love me."

"I swear it upon my heart," Lionus' voice was breaking. Eleni smiled weakly, but amidst that weakness, it was the most steadfast smile she had bestowed upon him. So much happiness entwined with her pain, it seemed as if the very strength of the gods coursed through her.

"I love you," she shivered. "It is cold."

Please do not leave me. You cannot do this to me. You cannot leave me here. Malefic, Aphrodicia – if either of you can hear me, help me. Gods, anyone!

"Never forget, you have a strong heart. You are the kindest knight in all of Emerion." Her head tilted back, her hand feebly clutching his. "The kindest knight." With those words, her eyes widened, and Eleni drew her last breath.

"No! No! NO! Curse Malefic! Do not do this to me!" but it was to no avail. Eleni now lay lifeless. As her grip relaxed on his arm, there was a tug at his back.

"Give me the ring, Lionus. It is not safe. They will come for you. They will *all* come for you."

"Darius, she is dead." *This cannot be. This cannot be.*

"She is with the gods now. Give me the ring. Save yourself."

But Lionus clutched his chest, gasping again, not from lack of air, but from the agony of losing Eleni. His chest tightened.

Darius merely stared at him. "It did not have to be like this, Lionus," he shook his head. "There is no saving you." Darius unsheathed his dagger and struck Lionus in the chest.

Pain seared through his ribs, as if a molten blade, forged with treachery, had been driven through him. Lionus gasped, and the world's blanket began to fall upon him. Chaos gave way to silence, and there was a tug on his neck. His head hit the dirt. He reached for Darius, scraping armor, but before he could snatch him, a dagger plunged once more into his chest. He gurgled, then coughed. In that moment, the pain, or the absence of blood in his body, caused the world to douse the flame of life.

CHAPTER 3: THE JEWEL OF EMERION

Lionus opened his eyes, a giant dragon skull hanging above him. All around, ruby and sapphire banners hung around the chamber, like sentinels guarding him… or preventing him from escaping. *The Valenour banners.* He began to rise, but a deep pain tore through his chest. "Ahh!" The pain caused him to fall back on the soft bed, Lionus clutching his chest. As he remained still to avoid aggravating his pain, he could not recall when he last slept in a bed this soft, let alone slept in one at all.

How did I get here? Where is Eleni? Darius? No. Was it but a nightmare? But he glanced around, and as he looked down at his chest wrapped in bloodied cloths, he knew it to be true. *Darius. You hound. You stole my ring. You abandoned Eleni and me. I should kill you. I will find you and make you regret it all.*

It was not long before the doors groaned open, a pair of guards stepping aside as a woman strode in.

She was a lean woman in an azure dress which matched her eyes. Her snowy hair in a lengthy braid running down her back made him instantly ask one question.

Is she a Valenour?

Wrapped in a fur cloak, she studied him, then took a seat beside the bed, keeping her distance. She maintained her shoulders back and sat with her spine erect, chin up. For a moment, she observed him, as if trying to learn all she could before he even spoke.

"Who are you? Where am I?" Lionus asked, cocking an eyebrow.

A lady's maid entered the chamber and stood by the lady beside him. "You are in Accreton, and I am the lady of the castle," she paused, her eyes lingering upon the hearth by the wall, before settling on him once more. "I wondered if you would awaken. I am glad to see you live. My maid will tend to you, and when you have regained your strength, we will speak. Rest now." With those words, she rose and departed the chamber.

Is that Valeciia? Why did she merely come if she was going to leave? Lionus leaned back as the maid brought a bowl of broth from the hearth. When he had finished, she tended to his wounds, crushing herbs and replacing his cloth. Not long after, Lionus fell into a deep slumber.

A week came to pass, the days blurred as Lionus slept away the pain, only wakening to see the maid tend his wounds and eat.

The doors to his chamber groaned as they opened. "Come," the servant said as he joined his side. "We must not keep the lady waiting."

"Where is she?" Lionus groaned as he propped himself on his elbow. The servant slipped an arm around him and helped him sit upright. He went towards a chair where a surcoat and fur cloak had been laid, gathered them, and returned to Lionus.

"The great hall. It is discourteous to keep the lady waiting."

"Then inform her I will be there swiftly." Lionus adjusted the cloth wrapped around his chest.

"She knows you will come. I am here to assist you in changing," he said, lifting the garments draped over his forearm.

Lionus' eyebrows furrowed. "I have no need of assistance in changing," but as he sat upright, he groaned. Though a week had passed and his pain had lessened, a cruel aching pain still lingered in his chest.

Lionus started to rise from the bed. As he did, the blanket slid down from his waist, exposing him. The servant kept watching him. "Are you certain you require no aid?" The servant's eyes flicked to another servant entering the chamber.

Lionus groaned. He huffed, then stared at the ground before him. *Cursed be Malefic. I would not be in this state if not for you, Darius. You traitor. I will find you. Perhaps getting out of this bed is the best for me. I need to move. I must meet the Lady of Accreton. Perhaps she can be of aid in finding this traitor.*

"Sir," the servant interrupted his thoughts.

Lionus shook his head, then looked up at him. He sighed. "I will require your aid in dressing."

The servant led him to the great hall. A lengthy stair led to the dais where three dragon-scaled thrones sat. In the center sat the Valenour woman who visited him in the chamber when he first awoke, the two flanking thrones vacant. A pair of quartered banners identical to the ones in the chamber hung behind the thrones. The wall was composed of dragon scales, and the more he stared at them, the sooner he realized he was truly in Accreton.

It is truly like the bard's stories. This place is... astonishing. The dragon thrones, made from real dragons, founded at the beginning of the Era of Ashes. If Eleni saw this, she would have loved it. Eleni... His nostrils flared, and Lionus stared at the dragons as if harnessing their power. *I will avenge us. Darius should have never abandoned us.*

The lady, upon seeing him, rose and descended the dais. It was not long before she made her cautious descent, one foot following the other. The aroma of beeswax and woodsmoke hung in the air, amplified by the heat emanating from the spiked braziers lining the sides. The hall, though it seemed desolate, was not, for lined along its sides were crested knights with ruby capes which seemed oddly familiar.

"Cretorian Guards. Three-throned dragon hall. Stained glass wall. This is certainly Accreton." Lionus' gaze darted to the woman. "You must be Lady Valeciia Valenour, the Jewel of Emerion."

Valeciia smiled warmly and bowed lightly. "A man who never missed a history lesson is welcome in any court. I trust your manners are as polished." Her smile faded as their gazes met.

Lionus took her hand and planted a kiss while clutching his chest. He was about to kneel when she stopped him. "Forgive me, my lady."

"There is no need to kneel, Sir?" she said while shaking her head.

"I am no knight, Lady Valeciia."

"A knight is a code, not a title." Valeciia smiled faintly.

Lionus stiffened as he looked up at her. *How does she know this? Was she in the inn? Or is she a mage able to read my thoughts?*

"Now what is your name?"

"Lionus, my lady."

She nodded. "I was there on the night of your grand gesture. You saved a man from certain doom, at the expense of your own."

He cupped his chin as he thought. *Why was Valeciia at the inn? It is unwise, particularly for a Valenour noblewoman, to be in such a place.* "Why were you at an inn and away from Accreton, particularly amidst these times when you are at war?"

Valeciia's gaze narrowed. "Walk with me." They strode the length of the great hall, then turned towards the gardens. Upon entering it, they were followed by a pair of guards. Valeciia and Lionus stopped by a stone bench, behind which stood a statue of Isabel Valenour on a rearing horse, bow aimed.

They were joined by a slender woman with caramel skin, chestnut locks cascading over her shoulders, and almond eyes. She wore an alabaster dress, her cloak fastened by a brooch shaped like a steed.

"This is Lady Agustina from the Silverlands," Valeciia said in a nonchalant tone, the young woman bowing as she met Lionus. "This is Sir Lionus, of Emeros."

Lionus frowned. *How does she know where I am from?* "I must be honest with the lady, I am no knight."

Valeciia rolled her eyes. "Guard, approach." The Cretorian Guard made his way towards her. "Your sword." The knight unsheathed his sword and handed it to Valeciia.

"Lionus of Emeros. I am making a humble request for you to serve as a knight under my banner. Will you accept?"

He stepped back, staring incredulously at Valeciia. *A knight…for a Valenour. Just so? She knows little of me. Whether I am of noble birth, or does she know more than I believe? She is aware I am from Emeros. Why is she doing this?*

Lionus smiled. "My Lady, I am humbled."

Valeciia shook her head. "It is but a simple request requiring a one-word answer. We are at war, and time is of the essence. Will you indulge me with a simple answer?" she asked while resting her hands on the pommel.

"Honored. I would be honored to serve the Jewel of Emerion," he said, nearly unable to get the words out. His skin tingled at the thought of being a knight.

Valeciia smiled when he gave his answer. "Kneel," and Lionus groaned while clutching his chest. One of the guards approached his side and aided him in kneeling. "Do you swear to protect the weak, protect my family, and serve with honor? To serve the call and guard the Valenour name until your dying breath or until you are released from oath, with all the honors and dangers it may bring forth?"

How am I even here? How is this happening? If Eleni had known I am on the verge of becoming a knight, her heart would swell.

He looked up at Valeciia, the lady awaiting her answer. "I swear it upon my heart, my lady." And the thought of his wife being there to see it caused his heart to come to a halt momentarily. But just as it halted, it sank to his stomach. *I may have failed you, Eleni, but I will not fail those whose lives I am sworn to guard under my newfound title. A knight is a code. I will bring us justice.*

"Then I dub you, Lionus, a Cretorian Knight of House Valenour." She tapped the sword on one shoulder, brought it over his head, and tapped the other, as was customary. "Rise, *Sir* Lionus."

The guard who aided him in kneeling assisted Lionus as he rose, Lionus groaning as he stood. "I am most grateful, Lady Valeciia. I must inquire, why have you chosen me, a stranger, as one of the nine?"

"Do you believe me a fool who chooses a man for such a position by chance?" Valeciia cocked an eyebrow while returning the sword to its former master.

"I would not dare," Lionus shook his head as he tugged on his fur cloak.

Valeciia merely laughed. "It is a jest, Sir Lionus. Lady Agustina will educate you on our court manners and jests. I would never leave chance to choose my most trusted warriors and confidantes. The nine Cretorian Knights are my most trusted soldiers. Beyond my prior knowledge of you, after witnessing your honorable trait with the man at the inn, and seeing your wife, with child, sacrifice herself to save you, I was aware there was no questioning your honor."

Sacrificing? She did not sacrifice herself for me. But the memories flooded his mind like a broken dam after a storm, and a lump caught in his throat. *How? Why?*

"Forgive me. Sacrifice?"

Valeciia glanced away. "You have no recollection. She used the ring's power to save you. You would have certainly perished if not for her. The Cretorian Ring is what saved you. She sacrificed herself so you could live."

He remained silent. *It cannot be.* "Why would she do this?"

"She loved you more than life itself. That is what true love is. There is no grander gesture of love than to sacrifice oneself for another."

But why? Why would she do this? I was meant to protect her and our family. I failed her. There was an ache in his chest. As if Valeciia sensed it as well, she placed a hand on his shoulder.

"The past cannot be undone. What we do with the future, however, lies within our grasp. Use it wisely, for not all are granted a second chance."

"I have nothing left. She was my everything. My life. My family. She was carrying my child," Lionus added. He trembled, then a jolt ran down his spine. It all returned to him.

After I broke the arrows' shafts on my back, Eleni touched me while wearing the dragon ring I had never seen before. That is why she was worsening despite having a less grievous injury. Then, she perished… and Darius arrived. He betrayed me, stole the Cretorian Ring I carried. I was betrayed by my own brother. He left me to die for a ring. For his ambition.

"Your friend never noticed the Cretorian Ring she carried. She had the healer's ring. It is one of the most noble of rings. To lose one's own essence to grant it to another? There is nothing more honorable than that," she said as she slipped the ring from her finger. Then, in her serene tone, she added, "I have wielded it in the past days to hasten your recovery as well. Nevertheless, I must confess, this was not the ring I sought at the inn," Valeciia glanced at the man beside her.

Lionus stared at his palm as she handed him the dragon ring with sapphire gems for eyes. *This was the ring Eleni wore to save me. This is all that remains of her.* Lionus looked up at Valeciia.

"I am most grateful. Yet I must ask, what ring were you searching for then?"

As if Valeciia caught a lump in her throat, she gulped. "The ring you had at the inn. It has many names. The Ring of Souls. The Ring of the Damned. The Ring of Judgement. It is unlike the one you possess. Instead of healing, it drains life from its source and restores the bearer. It is a perilous ring. It must be found."

"This is why I must be your Cretorian Knight. This is the reason for me to join you, is it not?" He stared at the woman as she nodded. There was a heaviness in his body, but in this moment, in this second chance at life, he knew what must be done. "Then I will serve you, my lady. Where do we begin?"

Valeciia smiled, rubbing his shoulder gently while she pointed at his hand. Her next words would bring his heart to a halt - words no mortal was ever meant to hear. "Wear the ring. It is time. It is time you tamed your dragon."

CHAPTER 4: DAMNED BE DALAX

Me? A Cretorian Knight. One of the nine mortals in all Emerion who gets to tame and ride a dragon, that is, besides the Valenours. Can it truly be?

"Once I tame the dragon, what is my task?" Lionus asked as they entered the pit.

"You will escort me to Argentum, the capital of the Silverlands," Agustina said.

Her forehead was beading with sweat, and Lionus could feel the same. It was uncertain how many dragons were being housed in the pit, but with the current war, he knew there were enough to lay waste to the entire kingdom. Lionus wiped his forehead as they continued walking within the pit.

"Do not fret, knight, you are not her caretaker," Valeciia winked at Lionus.

"Precisely. *I* will be your caretaker," Agustina chuckled, her arm intertwined with Valeciia's as they entered the pit.

"A jest, Lionus," Valeciia added. "Word has reached us that our Ring is in the Silverlands. Agustina will ensure you are cared for and guide you through any political hindrances that may arise throughout your journey."

"Besides, father expects me. A dragon ride shortens my travels," Agustina said, shrugging as she released herself from Valeciia's arm and continued pacing ahead.

"You do not fear dragons?" Lionus asked as they ventured deeper within the tunnels. *How does she not fear these treacherous beasts?*

Torches and fire pits ignited the way, the rest swallowed by the shadows of night. Low groans and grumbles came from ahead, above, and below, with the occasional pit master yelling at the beasts. Lionus followed her cautiously, yet within those pits, vigilance proved harder than expected.

"I lost my fear of dragons ages ago. Why would I fear one now?" Agustina rolled her eyes.

"Because there is one behind you… and it looks quite famished." The hairs on Lionus' nape rose. *By the gods! It is huge!*

Agustina halted in her tracks, then glanced back, the giant dragon baring its teeth at her. Its mouth caught aflame.

"Move!" Lionus jerked her arm and pulled her away.

They fell on the floor, Lionus groaning as Agustina collapsed upon him, the dragon's jaw snapping in their direction. With Agustina over him and his heart pounding, he understood why, of the few who became riders, fewer still survived.

Valeciia stepped between them, a pit master moving to intercept the beast. "Miscereg!" Valeciia raised her hands at the animal, "Miscereg!"

The beast came to a halt, its flame vanishing. It retreated deliberately into the shadows, eyes locked upon Lionus and Agustina as they lay sprawled out on the ground.

Valeciia pivoted to them, frowning. "Just because you carry a ring, does not mean dragons will not attack you. You are not a Valenour pureblood. The moment you remove that ring, you are the beast's prey. Even with it, you cannot truly tame it. You merely have control over its urge to decimate you," Valeciia said.

Lionus' chest rose as he inhaled, Agustina's heart racing against his, her palm on his chest. Lionus grabbed her hand and lifted it to ease the pain in his chest. Though Valeciia had healed him in the past days with the Cretorian Ring, he had yet to fully recover from his wounds.

"Get up," Valeciia said.

Agustina looked at Lionus, her hair disheveled while she panted. "Forgive me, Sir Lionus," she said as she got off him.

Lionus grimaced and offered her his hand, yet the fear etched upon her face seemed unlikely to fade anytime soon. Her alabaster dress had become filthy with the pit's dirt, and though she brushed it off, it was irremediable.

"All is well," Lionus added as he caught his breath, "will you be all right?"

"I am fine. I am all well," but the shrillness in her voice said otherwise.

"This is your beast, Lionus," Valeciia said.

The dragon crept out of the shadow once more as they backed away. Its eyes blazed with hatred for the world, and though it was not the biggest he had ever beheld, he knew it was a creature of fierce temper. Its scales matched his hair, obsidian in nature, and its underbelly a copper hue, with occasional streaks of the same color running alongside its snout and wings. Its thick wings led the way, the beast craning its neck. Lionus shuddered as he approached Valeciia, standing beside her.

"Tell Dalax, Miscereg. It means to calm down," Valeciia said.

Am I fit for this dragon, or will Dalax swallow me whole? Look at the size of it. One swift motion, and it will swoop down, and these pits will become the last sight any soul will behold of me.

Lionus held his breath momentarily and with an outstretched hand, said, "Miscereg, Dalax." The beast growled. *This may be the end of me... No. I will tame it. I have the Cretorian Ring.* But as he stared at the beast's eyes, even he struggled to believe his own words.

"Louder," Valeciia said. "Command him. Demonstrate you are his rider."

"Miscereg, Dalax!"

The beast halted, then growled deeper. Its eyes ignited, as if fury was brewing within once more.

I do not believe he wants to be ridden by me.

His hand shook lightly, but Lionus made a fist and extended it once more towards the beast.

I am its rider.

His hand ceased shaking.

Dalax bared his teeth once more and snapped at him.

Lionus leapt back.

You will not swallow me.

He commanded the dragon once more, "Miscereg, Dalax." The dragon's eyes became fixated on his hand, as if it noticed the ring. It sniffed, as if a scent were emanating from the ring. Then it became silent, as if the ring had a scent that caused it to cease its quest to devour Lionus.

"Good! Now to bond, say Vincalum," Valeciia whispered.

Lionus approached the dragon, "Vincalum, Dalax."

The animal lowered its head, nostrils flaring. As Lionus drew nearer, it bared its teeth once more.

It is going to devour me.

"Vincalum," he repeated. "Miscereg."

The dragon's flaming eyes stared at him, with an utter hatred within them that Lionus believed he would not lay a finger on the beast. But with each step, its breathing decreased, the beast deliberately hiding its teeth. It was then that Lionus knew he must touch it.

It seems it might not devour me after all. Is it truly listening to me, or is it just a ruse to win my trust so I might lower my guard?

Then, in one swift move, he laid his hand upon it, and the beast growled.

"Gently," Valeciia said.

"It tisn't some brothel whore." The pitmaster laughed.

"Vincalum, Dalax." Lionus stroked the dragon gently. The beast eyed him, and in an instant, its fury vanished. It closed its eyes, then rested its head on the ground.

Have I done it?

"Mount it," Valeciia said.

Lionus, however, was careful.

Should I mount it so swiftly? I have scarcely laid a hand upon it. He glanced at Valeciia, but she merely nodded as if she had read his mind. He held onto the beast's scales and clambered onto its back. *These scales feel impenetrable. This is why we rarely hear of these beasts' deaths.* When he made it to the top, he glanced at the women below and held onto the scales. *I am alive. I made it. I am on top of a dragon. Is this truly real, or is it merely a dream?*

He watched the women in the pit below, his jaw agape, the dragon side-eyeing him, as if it was contemplating whether Lionus should ride him or not. "Join me, Agustina." *Eleni. If you could see this. Who would have imagined I would mount a dragon?*

Agustina shook her head, the beast staring at her.

"Miscereg, Dalax." Lionus waved Agustina over, and after hesitating, she stepped to the side while the creature's gaze followed her. It was not long before she joined him, saddling herself before him on the beast. She was tremulous, just as Eleni had been the last night he was with her.

Is it this simple? A couple of commands, and we can fly as well? We are atop it. We must fly now.

"I will care for you," he whispered. Then to Valeciia, "How do we fly?"

"Volarze!" Valeciia said.

With that, the beast surged forward before Lionus could grasp it firmly or issue a command. The hairs on his nape rose as the beast moved.

"Hold on!" Lionus yelled.

Wing over wing, it snaked through the pit, searching for the light at the end of the tunnel. It flapped, flapped, then leapt from the edge of the plateau, plummeting to the world below.

"Ah!"

The beast fell, its wings unable to hold it in the air, the pair holding on firmly to the dragon's scales. Lionus' heart leapt to his throat, and the dotted trees grew with every second that Dalax's wings failed to lift them into the air. Agustina's screams rang out, and he was certain this dragon knew not the art of flying.

"Volarze, Dalax!" He had heard the tales in taverns of Dalax, and as it continued its descent, he realized this must have been how his last rider met his doom.

Flap! Flap! Flap!

The beast continued, but its descent did not end. The trees were about to hit their faces, and he knew this was how he would meet his end.

No. No. No. Rise, Dalax. This cannot be our end!

In the last instant, Dalax spread his wings wide, and he straightened. Trees under him snapped and tore against his underbelly. Lionus and Agustina held on tight, the air caressing his skin, the sweet air as the beast leveled. Dalax glanced to the side, as if he was enjoying teasing them in their fall.

"You are Malefic's dragon for certain," Lionus eased his grip on the scales.

The dragon let out a roar, a roar Lionus would never forget. Dalax's roar rumbled through eternity that day, and the world would come to know it as the day he acquired a new rider... or at the very least, his next victim.

CHAPTER 5: GUARDIANS OF ARKERON

Dalax soared eastward, towards the mountains beyond Goldcrest. Lionus clutched onto the reins. When he sought to guide the dragon, Dalax disregarded his command.

Where is he taking us? What other words can I use to command it?

Before he could command the beast, the dragon furled its wings and speared down. Lionus' mouth dried as the wind beat his face, Agustina's hair striking his face. Dalax continued his descent, Lionus tugging back… but Dalax paid him no heed.

The world below drew closer, the trees coming into view, and the snowcapped mountain growing with each moment.

"Rise, Dalax, rise!"

Yet the beast pressed on toward the mountainside. There was a waterfall along its side, the sun's rays glistening against its water. Lionus was blinded as they continued their approach.

Dalax is going to kill us both. He desires to make us his next victim.

They closed in on the mountain… *This is it. We are doomed.* The waterfall was ever closer. Agustina shrieked. Lionus closed his eyes and held on tight.

Dalax spun.

Then, the world went dark.

His growling reverberated.

A dampness was in the air.

The sounds of rocks crashing around continued.

This is it. We have met Malefic.

Then, everything came to a halt.

There was a flash of light, and Lionus opened his eyes. They found themselves surrounded by rock, a pair of braziers igniting an archway where two guards in plate armor flanked a priestlike figure. The three watched them intently, Dalax lowering his head as he moved to the side.

The priestlike man came forward, ebony cloak and hood concealing his figure. "Good, you have arrived as Lady Valeciia mentioned." He approached the dragon, and Dalax bared his teeth, but the man paid him no heed.

Who is this man? Where are we? Why has Dalax brought us here? Did Valeciia truly tell this man we were coming?

Dalax drew his head aside from the man's path, and once the figure had passed, Lionus arched an eyebrow. *Dalax is not attacking him.* Lionus glanced at the man's hands, but the man had no rings.

He is no Cretorian Knight. Who is he? Why does Dalax not attack him?

The figure stopped beside the beast. "Welcome to Talonspire. The name is Oculus, Ashscholar of the Guardians of Arkeron."

Guardians of Arkeron? I believed they were merely tall tales.

After a brief pause, Lionus dismounted Dalax, groaning as he made it to the ground. He aided Agustina in her descent, then the pair turned towards the man. The man smiled at them, his lips dry, his eyes hidden under the shadow of his hood. His cloak was clasped by a silver sun brooch, and as he turned, embroidered on his cloak, he had a ruby-colored dragon claw, open and poised, above which floated a sun identical to his brooch.

He began to walk away, and he nodded at the pair of guards by the archway. The men marched past him, clad completely in plate armor, ebony capes draped over their armors. They wore a barbuta helmet with a cream crest that flowed as they passed by Oculus. As they made their way past Lionus, he noticed the pair had on their capes the same insignia as Oculus' cloak.

Lionus and Agustina followed the man through the archway, and as they entered the second area of the mountain, he came to a halt and turned. Behind them, there was a rumbling sound, and the platform descended, Dalax vanishing with the guards into the depths of the mountain.

Where are they taking Dalax? I should not have come here. Yet, it was Dalax who brought me, and he himself seemed at ease.

Oculus reached toward Lionus. "Your Cretorian Ring, if you may."

What? My ring? I cannot give him my ring. I will not give him my ring. Lionus clenched his hand around it, turning the ring on his finger.

"If we are to safeguard you here, I will require your ring. It is secure with us. We are under Valeciia's watchful eye. We are The Ancient Valenoriian Order, the last known remnant of The Ancient Melanoriian Order."

What are these orders? How can I trust him? I merely met him. I cannot simply give him my ring because he requests it.

"No." Lionus' grip tightened on his sword's pommel.

Oculus remained silent, and he eyed Lionus' hand. Then, his hood lifted as he looked up at him, though Lionus still could not discern his eyes. "Good. A wise Cretorian Knight. You have passed your first test. Never surrender your ring to another living creature. In this world, power is your lifeline. That ring is your power."

Oculus smiled, then turned. Beyond the archway, a bridge stretched, and across it lay the entrance to a fortress carved within the mountain. Four guards stood watch, armored identically to the two they had encountered moments earlier. Oculus continued walking.

Lionus glanced at Agustina. She shrugged, and he eased the grip on his pommel. *What is this place? Where are we?*

"I always believed the tales of the Guardians of Arkeron to be tall tales. What purpose do they serve?" Lionus finally asked as they began to cross the bridge.

Under them, there was a shriek, and a flame shot into the air beside them. There were grunts and commands, Lionus peeking over the side of the bridge. *Dalax!* The men were escorting him through a tunnel under them.

Oculus spun, then remained staring at Lionus. "The most vital order in our world. We guard the portals to Arkeron, Malefic's Inferno," he leaned in, then his voice rose, "could you imagine the foul creatures escaping Malefic's Inferno into our world?" He shook his head, then clicked his tongue. "It would herald the end of our world, or, at the very least, cast us all into a living inferno. A plagued world. No. No, I could scarcely begin to imagine it."

Those creatures loose in Emerion. It would be the end of us. Dragons have brought such peril, but Malefic's creatures... no, that would certainly be frightening!

"But you stated you belong to the Order of Valenoriia. Do you not serve a second purpose?" Lionus tilted his head.

Oculus continued his march. The guards stepped aside, pushing the pair of metal doors, upon which was engraved the figure of Malefic, the ruler of Arkeron, standing with a snake coiled about his neck while he bore his golden spear.

They entered the fortress, and before them, a dragon statue made of stained glass stood with its neck craned towards the entrance, its wings spread wide until they brushed the walls of the domed room. A ray of light descended from the crown of the dome, striking the dragon and setting the chamber aglow.

"Is it-" Lionus began.

"A statue of the diamond dragon of Valenoriia," Oculus walked around the statue. "That is our second purpose, to seek the relics and the lost city of Valenoriia. As the last known sect, the history of the Melanoriians belongs in our stewardship."

And so the tales of the Guardians of Arkeron had proven true. There had been whispers of a brotherhood that safeguarded the folk of Emerion from the evils of Arkeron, even as they sought the lost city of Valenoriia. Now, before him stood the very seekers few had ever believed existed.

Lionus admired the statue resembling the diamond dragon of Valenoriia, the one ridden by the first Talon King, the Melanoriian often blamed for the sudden demise of the majority of the Melanoriian race.

They continued beyond the domed room, past a second set of doors with a diamond dragon engraved on it.

They entered the great hall, its vaulted spine arching high above. On both sides of the nave, the floor rose in lengthy, elevated tiers. A pair of stone stairs led to these flanking galleries. They did not, however, meet the nave at the entrance, but instead at the far end near the dais, after any newcomer who had traversed the nave had been carefully judged by the onlookers in the tables above.

Behind the dais, a pair of ebony banners hung high, bearing the claw and sun from Oculus' cloak. From the dais, a mirror shimmered, and Lionus' jaw fell agape. Except it did not offer a reflection, but a glimpse of a land beyond. From it, torches flickered in a chamber lined with the familiar Valenour banners, and as the light wavered, from within came the same woman who had knighted him.

Is that a portal? Did Valeciia just travel through a portal from Accreton?

Valeciia strode down the stairs leading to the dais, her dress' hem sliding carefully over the weathered stones, as if being cautious not to erode it further. The group reached her, and she eyed them.

"Oculus, you have arrived precisely as intended," she said as she met them at the foot of the stairs leading to the dais.

"And not a sand of time later," he bowed.

"Come." Valeciia led them up the stairs toward the left gallery and beneath an arch that carried them behind the wall protecting the dais. "This is the Survivor's Hearth, where our Guardians of Arkeron gather after their adventures, or after long and weary days of toil."

The chamber bore the same vaulted ceiling as the hall, as though it were an extension of it. It was lined with the banners of the Ancient Valenoriian Order, yet evenly spaced and intercalated with banners of the Valenours of Accreton. At the center burned a long fire, lined with chairs and men recounting tales in low murmurs, while others erupted in raucous laughter. Along the right side stood several tables where a cluster of armored men sat huddled together, as if sharing secrets of ancient relics long lost to time and merely known to them. Tables with arms, weapons, and shields were against the posterior wall, where two doorways stood at both ends.

A man from the long fire, upon noticing Valeciia, leapt to his feet and wobbled over to her. "My lady," the rosy-cheeked man said.

"Belkfor, son of Beavis. I pray you come bearing good news," Valeciia said as the plump man smiled at her, his wooden leg thudding upon the floorboards.

Is it truly him? The son of the man who reforged Isabel's Melanoriian Steel Sword? The one who added the emerald stone?

Few men possessed the ability to forge and shape such steel, and many claimed one must be born with hands touched by magic, for if one was not of Melanoriian blood, only a rare few were said to hold the craft required to fashion such weapons.

"Aye, my lady," he said while leading her towards the table in the back. The sound of metal scraping echoed as he rummaged through the weapons while they stood in wait. At last, he faced them, lifting a sword sheathed in a leather scabbard with a carved dragon.

Valeciia unsheathed the sword, its blade glimmering as its guard was shaped into a pair of feathered wings, the steel glimmering under the torchlight. Unlike Isabel's sword, which had an emerald on its pommel, Valeciia's sword had a dragon's tail at its end. She touched it with care, wincing as the blade pricked her finger. Then she smiled. "Vitarignis is sharper than ever."

Valeciia returned the sword to Belkfore, then pivoted to Lionus. "Before we get your Cretorian Knight's armor, Belkfore will repair your previous armor."

Belkfore? One of the greatest smiths in Emerion will repair my armor? This must be a dream. "I will have it brought to him."

"No need," Valeciia replied, then smiled lightly, "my people will fetch it. Now we have more pressing matters. You will continue to be tended by our healers," and she nodded towards the back of the castle, "and then you will begin your formal dragon training."

CHAPTER 6: AN UNEXPECTED VISITOR

Two months had come to pass, and Lionus was able to move about without any pain. He had finished sparring in the training yard, and he sheathed his sword as he walked away from his fellow combatant. Agustina had come to watch, and she sat on a bench beside the yard as Lionus made his way to her.

"Impressive agility," Agustina said as he joined her and removed his helmet, holding it against his hip.

"The lack of pain certainly aids the return of my agile steps," Lionus smiled.

"Will you visit Dalax now?" Agustina rose from the wooden bench.

Lionus snatched a tankard from a table beside her bench and chugged the ale. "I will be making my way there now." He placed the tankard down. "Will you be joining me?"

"Me?" Agustina pursed her lips.

"Aye, you rode Dalax once with me. Will you not join me?"

Agustina pressed a finger against her lips while looking up at the sky in a pensive state. She looked at him and paused briefly. "Let us not keep Dalax waiting."

They exited the castle's training yard and entered the dragon pits behind the fortress. Lionus led a sheep along with him, guiding it towards the entrance of a cave, the warmth emanating from within striking his face. The cave was covered in shadows, yet a low, distant rumble echoed through its depths. As they approached, the scraping of dragon scales against the ground brought him to a halt.

Lionus turned to the sheep, then slapped its hindquarters, the sheep rushing towards the cave. They stepped back and hid behind a wall in the cave. The sheep wheeled about and bleated, fleeing towards the entrance. Lionus held his breath as the scraping sound quickened, and the grumble rose.

Agustina edged back against the wall beside him, standing so close to him that he could feel her flowery scent.

A roar erupted, then a giant flame swept past them. Lionus' forehead beaded with sweat. The scraping of claws against the ground grew louder, and Dalax's breathing closed in. The beast brushed past the wall, knocking down stones as its wing slid past it. Then, Dalax snatched the sheep and darted back into the cave. He was about to go past them, but he came to a halt. His fiery eyes focused on Lionus and Agustina. He turned towards the two, the sheep's blood trickling from between its teeth.

What have I done? I came here simply for Dalax to swallow us whole.

The beast stared at them, sniffing Lionus. Blood dripped from its maw and onto Lionus' chainmail armor. Then, it huffed and shifted, continuing its path deeper into the cave.

"I believed it would devour us," Agustina fanned a hand to her chest.

"It seems our simple sacrifice has aided in gaining his favor," Lionus moved away from the cave's wall and glanced at the beast.

Dalax's flame had ignited a brazier nearby, and the dim glow now cast lengthy shadows along its face and horns. He swallowed the sheep in a single motion and coiled about, its fiery eyes fixed upon Lionus.

Agustina emerged from behind the cave wall and stared at Dalax, "It seems so," she glanced at Lionus, "I do not believe I have ever been this near a dragon. The one time I have had this opportunity was with you in Accreton."

Well, perhaps we can change that. "Come," he said while stepping toward Dalax, "let us change that once more."

"Are you certain?" Her hands shook.

Lionus nodded, taking a step before her, as if his body would be able to contain Dalax's flame and protect her.

"My husband loved dragons," Agustina said as she advanced toward him. Her hands remained shaking, and she hid behind Lionus as the dragon eyed them while they approached. "He always wished to see one in person, yet dragons seldom flew in the Silverlands."

"And is he back home in the Silverlands?" Lionus asked as they reached Dalax. The dragon held its gaze upon them, its fiery eyes tracking their every movement.

"I fear not. He is no longer with us. His dream of meeting or touching a dragon will never be fulfilled." She stared at the floor as Lionus looked back at her.

What happened to him? Did he die of the plague? A war? Famine?

"My wife, Eleni, loved dragons as well. She never truly had the opportunity to touch one. We once saw one fly over Emeros, but that was ages ago."

Agustina looked up at him "Really? How was it?" Her eyes widened.

"Dark as the night's sky. It was but a shadow crossing over the moon, but we saw it, and knew it was as beautiful as seeing a falling star," he said.

It feels like yesterday that we beheld on in flight, and today I am feeding one. How swift the world is to change our fates.

"I can see why one would never forget it," she said, her eyes gleaming under the brazier's dim light.

Lionus nodded, then took her hand, "Your husband may not have touched one, but perhaps you may live his dream once more, and relive the memory as if it were his own." Lionus guided her hand towards Dalax.

The dragon stared at them, its eyes darting to and fro from Lionus to Agustina. *I pray he does not eat her hand.*

Agustina's hand was shaking, and Lionus' own began to tremble. Agustina bit her lip, blinking rapidly as he brought her hand close to the dragon's scales. Dalax huffed, and Agustina leapt back.

"Ad rotium, Dalax," Lionus said to the beast, Dalax's nostrils flaring. "It means at ease," Lionus glanced at Agustina while taking her hand once more. "Do not fear. He will not harm us," though Lionus was uncertain if Dalax would truly not swallow them whole.

Agustina hesitated. She inhaled, then gulped. After sighing, she neared the beast once more. Lionus placed her hand gently over the dragon.

Dalax looked at her, and she shook, but Lionus tapped her hand gently. She met his gaze, then her eyes flicked back to Dalax.

"All is well. All is well."

"He trusts me. He trusts us," Agustina grinned as her eyes sparkled. She giggled and caught herself, covering her mouth, and Lionus could not help but laugh.

"It seems so, it seems so," he added. *Dalax seems to be warming up to us, or at the very least, tolerating our existence.*

That day, Lionus would learn how to guide Dalax to shoot streaks of fire. It was a day he would never forget, much like the night with Eleni when they saw the dragon fly past the moon.

After training, they returned to the Survivor's Hearth. They sat at a table set with a trencher of apples and pears, while they ate their broth stew filled with chopped pork, accompanied by a side of bread.

Briefly afterwards, the portal activated, and an elder with a snowy beard and matching wavy hair arrived, wearing a charcoal cloak. He sat with Oculus in the great hall, the pair musing over a map he had found. They were joined by a Talonseeker, one of the warriors dispatched to the field to search for relics, and an Ashkeeper, a member of the lowest rank amongst the Guardians of Arkeron who learned under the guidance of scholars or whichever guardian he was assigned to. The pair wore the same robes as Oculus, though fashioned of wool and roughly sewed, for the Ashkeeper scratched at his sleeves incessantly as he watched the map.

Lionus watched through the archway leading to the great hall, and after the men mused over their newest finding, a Guardian of Valenoriia, the rank assigned to the same men who escorted Dalax when he first arrived at Talonspire, joined them.

The robed man looked over Oculus, and he noticed Lionus watching him. Lionus tore his gaze away. The men began to mumble, and the elder made his way to Lionus' table. Agustina glanced up at him, and the fellow nodded.

"You must be the Cretorian Knight Valeciia has brought to

train," the man said in a hoarse voice, his hazel eyes narrowing as he studied Lionus and pointed to the seat beside them. "May I join you?"

"Any friend of Valeciia is a friend of ours," Agustina said before Lionus could answer. "Come sit," she patted the bench beside her.

Who is this man?

The man sat beside Agustina and looked at Lionus, then smiled. "The name is Kronac, and my fate with the Valenours has brought me here once more."

Once more? What does he do for them?

"I am Lionus, and she is Agustina," Lionus said, then continued to eat his soup.

"I was made aware. Your fate with the Valenours has been sealed for quite some ages now." *My fate?* An Ashkeeper came his way and handed him a tankard with ale. Kronac nodded at him, and the young lad rushed away. "Do you believe in fate, Lionus?"

Fate? What is fate? Was it fate for Eleni to perish? For me to find the Cretorian Ring so that I could become a dragonrider? If this is fate, then the gods are cruel with their wicked games.

"At times, I wish I did not." Lionus eyed his tankard.

"I see." Kronac paused. He looked at Agustina, "Have you heard the stories of Valenoriia?"

Agustina beamed as she put her stew down and met his gaze. "How could I not? The grandest romance story of all time!"

Kronac chuckled, and Lionus looked up at him. "Indeed, yet the Fall of Valenoriia has brought us together. It is our fate, we were destined, to be here in this very moment together. As were those lovers destined to fight for one another, bringing the Melanoriian race to the brink of ruin. Were it not for them, what would have become of the world? Had but a single moment in history been altered, the entire course of our own might not have come to pass," he stopped, then sipped his ale. Kronac faced Lionus, "Do you not believe it so, *Cretorian Knight*?"

One alteration and we could have ceased to exist. But one moment could have spared an entire race. Perhaps the survival of one meant the fall of another. "Perhaps. Perhaps not."

Kronac shook his head, "Believe it, Lionus, for I have met the maker of the destiny you are currently living. As much as the Talon King and his lover's fate was intertwined during the Fall of

Valenoriia, yours is intertwined with the Valenours, like a snake around a branch on the verge of eating a mouse. The question remains, are you the snake, or will you be the mouse?"

What? Me? My fate intertwined with the Valenours? This man is mad. Is he a god? Has he met the god who forged my future?

"Who are you?" Lionus cocked an eyebrow and clutching his tankard.

The man shook his head, "I am no one. I am simply a man on his travels, who is sought for stories and maps in trivial and grand courts alike. I am a man often better left forgotten." Kronac took a final sip of his ale as he rose. He placed the tankard on the table, then cast one last look at Lionus, "You have not yet begun to live, Lionus. You have barely begun to live your fate. The question you must dig to find, buried deep within you, is: who are you? Who will you truly become?" And with those words, he walked away before Lionus could answer.

As he left the Survivor's Hearth, Lionus wondered if he would ever see the man again. *Then was losing Eleni all fate? Was she meant to be killed in this manner so I could become another man? Was I meant to suffer the loss of the woman I loved, for what, for joining the Valenours' path? Indeed, who am I then? Who will I become?* Yet of all the questions he had, one plagued him most. *Who was Kronac?*

"Who was that man?" Lionus said while shaking his head. "I must drown this terrible dream," and he gulped what was left of his drink.

"Kronac," Agustina said, then reached for his hand. Lionus met her gaze, a curiosity and happiness within them he could not begin to unravel, like a child receiving its first gift during the winter celebrations of Yoyam. "I have seen him, on occasion, speaking with the Valenour children. They seem to adore him and always wish to see more of him. The older Valenours call him wise, others mad."

"I can certainly see why." *Why does he speak often to the Valenour children? Why do they wish to see more of him?*

"Few know much about him. A wanderer of the courts and the world, they say, a bard with stories of Valenoriia and Valenours past, though he seldom speaks of anything besides Valenoriia," Agustina said, then bit her lip while she looked down and stirred her soup.

"A man who speaks so much of Valenoriia, yet little is known about him. Does that not make you uneasy?" Lionus stroked his beard.

"Never has he given me cause for unease." She stopped stirring her stew. "There is, nevertheless, one thing about him."

Lionus met her gaze, "What might that be?"

She stared at him before answering. "Kronac has never spoken falsely. Whoever he may be, of this one truth we must be certain: your destiny is bound to this family, and you will walk hand in hand with the Valenours."

CHAPTER 7: ZAN ROSEA

Four more months had come to pass while Lionus remained in Talonspire learning to ride Dalax. When his training was complete, he flew to the Silverlands to fulfill the quest Valeciia had entrusted him with.

As Dalax ascended to the clouds, Lionus' heart steadied. Agustina's own heart calmed against him, her muscles relaxing as she found peace nestled in the corral created by his arms. Lionus held the reins firmly, his arms tense as the beast flew, hunched over, hoping the wind would not cast him from the saddle. As Dalax tore through the clouds, a cold sensation brushed over Lionus' skin. Agustina's back crashed against his chest as she trembled, and she glanced back at him.

"Forgive me. It is not a daily occurrence to find oneself among the clouds," she tugged her cloak.

"There is nothing to forgive," Lionus tugged on the reins to bring Dalax lower.

As if she found comfort in his words, Agustina smiled, and she spread her arms as if she was attempting to catch the cloud's cold embrace.

Lionus could not help but smile at the gesture, yet it quickly faded when Dalax glanced aside as a swooshing sound emerged from the clouds above.

An ashy dragon, thrice the size of Dalax, appeared. Its scales were scarred, some scales missing, a testament to its war-hardened history. The beast glared at them, but Dalax remained steady in his flight, baring his teeth.

Lionus' heart hitched, and Agustina shrank between his arms, as if seeking to be caged and shielded within them.

I was trained to fly and attack, but I have not yet fought another dragon. How will I fight it? How do I protect Agustina?

Upon seeing the silver-haired woman with the familiar fur cloak atop the dragon, Lionus' grip on his reins eased. *Valeciia. What is she doing here?*

"It is Valeciia," Lionus said to Agustina.

A sigh of relief escaped her. "I had nearly forgotten she would fly to escort us to my family's abandoned fort."

And so Valeciia did. As they neared the fortress and plunged toward it, Valeciia peeled off. They descended, Dalax halting as his wings flapped forcefully over the battlements. The woods behind the fortress shook, as if fleeing his arrival, until the beast landed within the courtyard of the ruined fortress.

Lionus dismounted the dragon and aided Agustina, guiding her safely to the ground. He gazed around and took her hand. "What was this place?" he asked as he wandered ahead of the dragon.

"Zan Rozea, the Fort of the Roses." She turned away and plucked a rose. Agustina gently removed the leaves before placing it on her hair.

"Watch the thorns," Lionus said as she finished tucking it over her ear. Agustina smiled, "The roses of Argentum carry no thorns. It is their unique beauty. It is said they were brought from the flying cities of the Melanoriians themselves."

"Those cities are myths, tall tales," Lionus crossed his arms and continued to admire the dilapidated fortress. Thatched roofs were now in disrepair, stones littered the ground, and weeds and vines were overgrowing the buildings scattered within it. Even then, few rose banners remained, their words tattered and lost to history.

"Are not all stories lost in history believed to be myths and tall tales? Were dragons not myths? The Valenour themselves?" Agustina asked as she led him towards a stable where a white mare stood unsaddled. Agustina reached for the leather saddle on the side, but Lionus stepped alongside her before she could grab it.

"Perhaps," Lionus took the saddle, "allow me," and he saddled the horse.

Agustina bowed lightly, and Lionus aided her in mounting.

Lionus and Agustina abandoned the forgotten ruins, galloping down the rose-filled countryside. Lionus had never seen so many roses, fields brimming in crimson, like a blanket laid upon the land. He brought the horse to a trot, his lips slightly parted as he admired the countryside. After they traversed the fields, they entered another forest.

"Help! Help!" a man called out within the forest.

Lionus unsheathed his sword. *Is it a cry for aid, or a trap?*

As they continued along the path, the voice grew ever louder. Suddenly, the voice was coming from above. Lionus searched the trees and found the culprit. A man in a russet tunic hung upside down, dangling from one leg as he was ensnared upon it like wild game. "I beg of you, help me." The man reached for the rope around his leg. He was a fair-skinned, blonde man with a merchant's guild ring on his finger, and he continued to sway in his desperate attempt to escape. "Could you release me? I will reward you. You can keep my silver ring. It is all I have left," the man continued to cry out to them.

"What happened?" Agustina said while Lionus carefully examined his surroundings.

Are we alone, or are they still here?

"It could be a trap," Lionus whispered, but as he searched, he found no other creature amongst them.

"Those thieves stole my horse and my coin. If not for the wolves, they would have butchered me and sold my skin to the nearest tanner."

The man recounted his story as Lionus approached him, a tear marring his tunic and a gash cutting across his cheek.

Perhaps he is not lying. It seems he may have truly been attacked.

Handing Agustina the reins, Lionus kept an eye on the man as he dismounted the horse. Lionus cut the rope. Behind him came a loud crash.

"Ow! A word of caution would have sufficed," the man said as he fell on his back and rubbed his arm.

Lionus shook his head and watched the man get up. The man, upon seeing his savior, quickly rushed toward him, arms spread wide. "Oh, may the gods bless you!"

Lionus lunged back while shaking his head. With his sword unsheathed, he pointed it, and the man retreated as the point met his neck.

"I meant no ill will." He slipped the ring from his finger. "The name is Wilken. Take this token of gratitude for saving me from certain doom."

Lionus glanced at the ring. It was certainly worth its weight in silver, particularly with the guild barrel emblem carved onto it. "Keep it."

Wilken's hazel eyes, identical to Lionus', widened. "How noble of you. Words of a knight," he brushed his clothes. "If I may ask, where are the lot of you headed?"

"That is a private matter," Lionus sheathed his sword.

Agustina, however, interjected, "Argentum."

"Ah, then would it be much to request an escort to Alzeriia? It is the town before it," Wilken said as Lionus returned Agustina.

"Certainly. It is on our way," Agustina added while looking at Lionus.

Lionus gripped the saddle. *We must make haste. We are on a quest.* Lionus did not wish to delay matters further in obtaining Argentum's lord's aid. But the look in Agustina's eyes was enough to deter him. Lionus sighed, and he was well aware that, in the end, Agustina would most likely not yield in her quest to aid the man. He was a knight, and even if he was away from Accreton, his oath to the people would terminate the day the sun rose in the west and set in the east.

"You can join us, but we have no mount for you," Lionus turned toward the man, his hand on his sword's pommel. *Even on a quest, escorting Wilken is the knight's way.*

"Oh, do not fret. I need the walk. It has been a long journey on horseback. Rest assured, your efforts will be rewarded," Wilken said, a glee of delight in his eyes.

They pressed onward until they reached the rivertown of Alzeriia. On its eastern border, the river ran its course, the remainder of the town flanked by the woods where they had found Wilken. Lionus paused to examine the town. Carts filled with logs were led by families as they entered the town. Chickens pecked at the ground around them, and children rushed joyfully through the roads. It was a sight unlike the war-torn world where Lionus had just come from. He could rarely recall the last moment when he had seen such joy.

Lionus dismounted the horse and led it by the reins. As Wilken led them towards the tavern in the center of town, there was a group of men huddled around a tangled mass of fallen trees, the earth torn where their roots had once held them fast. They had fallen on the road leading south, away from Alzeriia. Lionus continued along the dirt path through the town, while observing the men around the trees. They were in low murmurous discussion, and as they saw Lionus approach them, they succumbed to silence.

"You seem like a sturdy fellow," one of the men said to Lionus, raising his axe over his shoulder.

"Just a man passing through," Lionus said while bringing the horse to a halt.

The men stared at each other, then the eldest in the group approached him. "Would you be willing to aid us? I must say, we cannot offer you much lad. Soup at the inn is all we can offer for your labour."

We must keep marching on to fulfill our quest. Nevertheless, we are to stay the night here. Lending these men our aid while we are here is the just course.

"I did not require payment, but soup will suffice." The men nodded in approval and returned to their work as Agustina watched with a faint smirk.

As Lionus aided the men in felling the trees, a sharp crack split the air. He looked up—then a snap! A lengthy branch swung down toward one of the villagers. "Watch out!" Lionus yelled, but before the man could turn to spot the incoming danger, Lionus leapt toward him.

Smack!

The branch struck Lionus. He flew, his back slamming against a cart. There was a tearing sound, and a shock of pain rushed up Lionus' back. The villager he pushed rose, then he and the other two men rushed toward Lionus.

"Are you injured?" they asked as Lionus rose.

Lionus groaned and reached for his back. His fingers brushed the jagged edge of the torn tunic. Lionus winced. Warm blood coated his fingers, and he wiped it on the grass beside him. "I will live," he said, nodding at the men.

They looked at each other wide-eyed. The man he saved then said, "Thanks for saving me, lad! If that tree had struck me, I would not have fared as you have."

Lionus placed his hand on the man's shoulder, "It was the noblest course."

The man smiled, then he turned to look at Lionus' back. "Seems but a flesh wound. Cleanse it well, or it will rot."

"I will make certain of it." Then, as if nothing had happened, he continued to assist the men.

Once he had aided in cutting the trees, Lionus placed the axe alongside a trunk he had carried. He wiped his forehead with his forearm, then parted towards the inn.

Agustina had been helping a woman carry water from the river, and as she finished, she joined him on his way to the inn. There, they took a room for the night, and Lionus stepped away to take a bath.

As he neared the wooden tub, the aroma of lavender took over the air. The door swung open, and he turned to see who had entered. "Agustina, what are you doing here?"

"You are going to take a bath. You need aid," Agustina replied while making her way to the table behind him.

"Certainly, but one of the ladies in the inn would undoubtedly suffice," Lionus said in an uncertain tone while turning away from the tub. *This is not customary in Emerion.*

"You would allow a stranger to bathe you?" Agustina cocked an eyebrow.

You are not a stranger, but we are not courting. This is a peculiar ask.

As if she read his mind, she continued. "It is Argentum hospitality. Since our times in the sky cities, we have always seen to our Melanoriian lords, ladies, and their warriors. This is the least I could do to serve you for returning me home and aiding the kind people of Alzeriia." She pointed to his side, "You certainly require more than a simple bath. I saw your injury. I must tend to your wound, or it will fester. My mother educated me on the healing properties of our herbs, a skill I doubt the ladies in the inn could match." Then, in a playful tone, Agustina added, "Rest, knight, I have not come to slay a warrior in your most vulnerable moment."

Lionus nodded, then removed his surcoat and entered the wooden tub. He cleared his throat. Lionus then spoke in a tone mimicking hers, though the feeling of having her beside him caused his muscles to remain tense, "How can I be certain you are no assassin?"

Her hand guided him to face forward as she placed a stool behind him. There was a scraping sound, followed by silence, and then a splash. Water rushed down his head. Lionus nearly leapt out of the tub when the icy sting bit his shoulders.

"An assassin would have a dagger to your throat, not running water down your head," Agustina chuckled.

"This water is certainly as deadly as any assassin's dagger," Lionus shivered. Just as he said this, a woman entered the chamber carrying a bucket of water and a cloth.

"The warm water requested, Sir Lionus," the woman said. Agustina called her over, water continuing to splash behind him, "and the cloth with your herbs, my lady."

Once she left, Agustina said, "I am certain I did not just hear a child's cry escape a Cretorian Knight. Do not fret, knight, you will not fade into Malefic's world due to a plunging in icy waters."

"I would certainly hope not." His muscles relaxed as she poured the warm water. "Quite a dull manner to leave this world."

"Ah, then I would imagine you have many tales of your adventures."

And so he did. He sank his hands into the water, the dragon ring still on his finger. Then, Lionus spoke of the many lands he had travelled in Emerion. Of battles, treasures, quests, and countless adventures he had. All the while, he recounted the numerous places any man could dream of going, places his sword and skill had allowed him to traverse while he earned his keep with his wife.

"I must ask," Lionus cocked an eyebrow, "you state you have not travelled much, yet you seem to be well acquainted with Lady Valeciia."

"We have known each other since we were children, not long after she crossed the Serene Sea with her mother," Agustina said while she passed a cloth over his shoulder, cleansing the dirt that had fallen on him while helping to carry the logs.

"I had heard Valeciia was such a kind and joyful woman. Was it truly as they said? She seemed quite serious," Lionus turned to look at her.

"She is, never has changed," Agustina said while moistening the cloth and squeezing the excess water, her gaze lingering on the tub, as if she was recalling days past. Then, she looked up at him, "War has a way of changing people. Now that she is the head of her family, she bears a more solemn demeanour." There was a pause. "Can you tell me more about your wife, Eleni? The way you speak of her… it is quite endearing."

Eleni. Who was Eleni? She was everything. Happiness. Joy. Strength. Everything. Now, just a mere reminder. Pain. How can I not speak of the woman I loved in such a manner? I still cannot believe… I cannot believe she is dead. What did they do with her corpse? I am certain Valeciia did not take her. She was left to Emerion, to nurture the ground where she came to pass.

"My wife… she was a wonderful woman." Though months had come to pass, there was a pressure on his chest, as if the thought of her brought Malefic to press his deadly hand upon a wound that would only heal entirely through time, if at all. "We fought in many battles, protected each other in quests all throughout the land ever since we left our home in Emeros. She was going to have my child, *our* child. Then, in our final battle, we were both injured…"

"Oh," she reeled away, as if she had committed the grandest of treasons in the realm. Her cheeks flushed with embarrassment, and Lionus took her hand gently, comforting her.

"That was the last time I laid eyes upon her." There was a heaviness in his chest, and he recalled how when he thought about it in Accreton, it was as if the weight of a thousand dragons was upon it. Now, the pressure lingered, but time had certainly eased the pain he had for his wife in those first days. *She was the light in my darkness. Life in a world riddled with death.*

"And… and…" She hesitated, as if she was wondering if she should pry further. Her gaze met his, and there must have been a calmness in it, as if his eyes alone could bring the end of a thousand storms, because she finally continued, "She passed away from her injuries, saving you, as Valeciia said?"

The weight in his chest eased, though his throat was dry. He still found it difficult to find the words to speak of his wife. He stared at his ring, and as if it lent him the strength, he said, "Aye. They killed them. An arrow to the belly. I could not save her, nor the child she was carrying," Lionus stared at the cloudy water. "Valeciia said Eleni sacrificed herself for me, with this ring. It is all I have of her… all which remains of that day." He removed the ring from his finger and turned it over in his hand, as if finding a magic area where he could release its energy. For a moment, he wondered if there was some way he could bring her back, but he quickly realized the world was not as magical… a fate sealed in blood could not be undone. While in Talonspire, Valeciia had told him he could heal with it at the peril of weakening himself, but no person could be brought back from Malefic's Portals.

"It is clear you loved her deeply. I am certain that you did all you could to protect her. Eleni knows, now that she is with the gods, that you did all you could for her," Agustina said while rubbing his back.

Lionus looked up at her, a weak smile on his lips. The pressure vanished from his chest, and he slid the ring back on his finger. With it, the thoughts of Darius betraying him returned. He recalled the sharp dagger striking his chest, and he formed a fist. *I thought you were my friend. My brother. Yet you betrayed us for a ring. For power.* Lionus' eyes narrowed as he looked at her, "Not all. Not all is done."

CHAPTER 8: A DANCE TO REMEMBER

Once Agustina cleansed his wound and he finished his bath, Lionus and Agustina went to the inn below. Wilken joined them, and the three shared a supper of pottage and sausages. A group of men sang in a corner, a man playing the lute while the men raised their mead-filled tankards in unison. It was a song Lionus had never heard, and from its verses, it seemed to tell of the first days of Argentum.

He never fully grasped its history, for they were joined by an ambassador with beady eyes and a lengthy beard wearing a lime tunic. The ambassador was followed by a husky, flame-haired, bearded man who was similar in height but wore a wool tunic stained with tree dust and a leather jerkin. He carried an axe, as though he had just finished chopping wood and come to the inn for his evening mead.

Lionus cocked an eyebrow. *Who are these men?*

As they approached, Agustina rose to greet them. "Lord Gervais," she said toward the ambassador, "Baldric," she looked at the man with the axe, "it is great to see the two of you here."

"We have missed you at court, my lady," Gervais said as he took her hand and planted a kiss upon it.

"There were matters which called me away from Argentum's court," Agustina replied. As she answered, Gervais glanced at the table where Wilken and Lionus sat.

"I would not expect otherwise. Your duties have always been of the utmost importance, whether within the court or beyond it. May we join you?"

"We would be delighted in your company," she pointed to the table as the men joined them. Lionus set down the tankard one of the barmaids had handed him as Agustina introduced the pair, the men exchanging greetings. "Baldric, word has reached me that you have a log cart bound for Argentum. Might there be room for a friend and her companion?"

"I would never deny you passage in my cart, my lady," Baldric said, stroking his beard. His gaze remained fixed on Lionus.

Gervais continued speaking, "We would also require a favor," and he turned to Lionus, "from your friend."

A favor? From me? Lionus brought the tankard to his lips and looked at the ambassador from behind the rim. "I no longer render mercenary services."

"Understood," Gervais' eyes locked on Lionus' ring, "a Cretorian Knight. I am certain few men would continue to render their services if offered to be knighted into the Valenours' order." Lionus brought the tankard down, then nodded as the man paused.

It is one of the most feared orders. Why would any man be a mercenary after becoming a Cretorian Knight?

Gervais continued, "Few Cretorian Knights make their way through these lands… if any at all. If you could spare me but a couple grains of sand from your hourglass."

But a couple of extra coins would not hurt my pouch. "I could spare a few."

"We bear a gift of great importance which must be delivered to Argentum. I share this only because of our trust in Lady Agustina and the reputation of the Cretorian Knights that precedes you."

A gift. Gifts that require being escorted are rarely simple gifts. Smells like danger. Smells like quite the quest.

"There is quite the recompense, if that is what you are wondering. It is well known that we offer generous rewards for our quests."

Agustina leaned in and whispered, "They are trusted friends of the family. I would not hesitate to say the recompense may outweigh whatever trouble they may bear upon us."

Coin. Same route. Possible danger. Agustina trusts them. I pray the gods I do not come to lament this decision.

Shaking his head and raising his tankard, Lionus said, "We are bound by honor," and the pair shook hands. The men rose from the table and joined the innkeeper.

As the men left, a barmaid handed Agustina a tankard of wine. She was about to take a sip when the men in the corner of the inn began a new song. Agustina squealed, Lionus turning with wide eyes and cocking an eyebrow. "That was unladylike of me," she said, covering her mouth. "Forgive me, Sir Lionus. It is simply one of my most beloved songs."

Wilken let out a laugh from the other side of the table, and Agustina began to move joyfully, her dress swaying from side to side. "I require a partner," she said, reaching out to the men.

Wilken shook his head, "Oh, my lady! As honored as I may be, I fear my cups have taken the best of me. Sir Lionus will join you!" he pushed the knight toward her.

"Oh, no. I seldom dance." Lionus raised his hands in denial, a heaviness settling in his stomach.

"Certainly. You preserve your talents for nights like these with beautiful Argentum ladies!" Wilken smiled and swayed his tankard to the rhythm of the lute.

Agustina, with an outstretched hand, said, "Join me, Sir Lionus. It is my most beloved song. Will you permit a lady to forego such an opportunity?"

Lionus took a deep breath as he glanced at Wilken, the merchant shrugging and leaping from the bench towards Agustina. He snatched her tankard and pulled Lionus up from his sedentary state toward her. Lionus took her hand, and Agustina's smile only brightened with the sight of the knight joining her. They snaked through the crowd, and before he knew it, Lionus had a hand on her waist, his other intertwined with hers as Agustina placed her hand gently on his shoulder, and they swayed near the hearth.

I have not danced with any other person since Eleni. Should I truly be dancing with Agustina?

The next song he heard was unknown to him, but it seemed as if most in Alzeriia had heard it. It was about a pair of lovers, a siren and a knight. As the song continued and the men in the inn sang, more couples joined the dance. The surrounding people caused them to come closer. As their bodies neared, Lionus glanced down at her, Agustina closing her eyes momentarily as she hummed the song the minstrels were playing. With every tune from the lute, they moved effortlessly, gradually moving ever closer.

It has been many moons since Eleni passed. It has been many moons since I lost her. Even then, this is merely a dance.

Around them, women leaned into men's chests, others gazing at each other happily while singing.

Is it truly evil if I tread a new path? If I enjoy this simple dance? It is merely a dance.

For a moment, the scent of flowers emanating from Agustina seemed to entice him. *I loved Eleni. I stood steadfast by her side. But now that she is no longer with me, is it wicked that I find myself beside Agustina?*

He lowered his chin, only to be met by Agustina lifting her head to look up at him. For a moment, his gaze lingered, fixed upon her almond eyes. Agustina did not suppress her sweet side, the corners of her eyes wrinkling as she beamed.

"And here I believed you were not a dancer," she said.

"My wife loved to dance," his words seemed to burn her, for her expression faded and she pulled away slightly. However, Lionus' hand was firm on her back as they twirled. The momentum brought her back, and simultaneously, Lionus could only recall his wife. *Eleni. How she would twirl. That woman carried the sun's energy. Such joy in her eyes.* The dull pressure in his chest resurged. Then, his eyes welled. He blinked it away hastily. *How could I lose her? The world does not feel the same without her. There is such a void without her.*

"Are you well?" Agustina leaned in.

"All is well," Lionus said, but his throat was dry, and the words came with effort.

There was a shriek, then a plop. Plates clattered. The music came to a halt. Lionus and Agustina turned in the direction of the turmoil. A couple of people huddled around their table. Lionus snatched Agustina's hand, her palms clammy, and they approached the table.

On the floor, he had foam in his mouth, blood in his eyes. Veins snaking throughout his skin. Then, more blood escaped through his nose. Wilken lay sprawled out on the ground. Dead. Screams reverberated throughout the inn. Men glanced at each other, and another dropped dead. Beside the dying pair, their tankards lay on the ground.

"Murderers!" a man yelled, and the people in the inn turned on each other. Yelling turned to shoving, then to daggers and swords.

Who did this? Who killed Wilken? Lionus was at a loss for words as he stared at him. He was about to close in on Wilken when someone tugged him. With eyes wide as shields, Agustina looked at him. Her hand, held firmly within his, was shaking.

Beside her stood Baldric, "Come, my lady and Sir Lionus. We must leave. An assassin is on the loose. We will get you to safety."

And as the inn broke into chaos, Baldric snaked Lionus and Agustina through the crowd.

Beside them, a man was shoved into a table. Another man rushed at Lionus, and Lionus gripped his sword's handle. But the man passed through, and Lionus' grasp eased as he brushed past him.

Lionus pulled Agustina closer, then wrapped his arm around her. She looked up at him, burying her head against his chest. He braced against the men pushing against them, then shoved a man with his free hand. The man crashed against a chair, and Lionus continued to rush through the crowd before he could rise and find them.

The trio made it outside, and as Baldric shut the door, a carriage pulled ahead. "Get in!" Baldric yelled as he rushed beside them.

Where are we going? What is going on?

But Baldric did not allow them to speak. He opened the door to the carriage, then pushed Lionus within. Before they could even begin to contemplate what had happened, they were on a carriage on their way to Argentum. Behind them, screams turned to echoes. Lionus' muscles relaxed as the screams eased, yet Agustina was shivering incessantly.

The echoes were drowned out by the forest's silence.

But silence was not all, for in the distance, the pounding of hooves drew ever nearer.

Is it the men from the inn after us?

Their driver, however, slapped the reins.

As Lionus looked through the carriage's side, there was a sudden whisper.

Thud! An arrow had flown past him and struck a tree. *Who are they? Why are they after us?*

In that moment, the race for survival began.

CHAPTER 9: HALL OF THE SUMMONED

Lionus reentered the carriage. "Do not peek out! We are being followed," Lionus said to Agustina. She merely sat there trembling, and Lionus took her hand. "We will survive. All will be well. I will protect you.

Agustina nodded, her trembling easing.

Lionus peeked out of the carriage and called out to the driver. "We are being pursued. Make haste."

The driver slapped the reins, the carriage accelerating. Lionus reentered the carriage, his back slamming onto the seat. He searched the carriage, but found no bow, nor any weapon he could throw. *We will have to sit this out or wait for them to close the gap.*

He continued to peek through the side of the carriage. Then, the sound of distant hooves vanished, and all that remained were the sounds of his driver commanding their horses.

They ceased their pursuit. Just like that?

Even then, Lionus kept a careful watch on the forest, but the riders never returned. Eventually, they arrived at Argentum, the sounds of hooves never rising again.

Towering walls extended into the sky from the forest below, torches evenly spaced throughout the battlement's length. The Silver Sea in the east could be heard lapping against the coastline, yet the sound of crashing waves was soon swallowed by the commands of the guards on the walls.

"Halt," the few moving torches along the walls came to a stop. Outside the carriage, footsteps approached the side of the reinsman, and there was a light murmur. After a brief pause, the footsteps came alive again. With every passing second, they grew louder. Lionus' gaze shifted between Agustina's darting glances and the door. *Will they allow us into the city?*

He took Agustina's hand quickly and tapped it gently, "Do not fret." She had calmed after their escape, but even then, she tapped her foot incessantly.

The guard's steps ceased, stopping outside the door. There was silence, then a click, and the carriage door swung open. The guard raised his torch, his eyebrows furrowed. "What brings the lot of you to Argentum this time of the night?" He was fixed on Agustina.

Lionus cleared his throat. "Delicate business."

The guard's attention shifted to him. "All delicate business goes through us," he extended his torch towards them.

Lionus leaned forward, and the torch's flame flickered on his ring. There was a momentary pause, and the man stepped back. "Welcome to Argentum, Sir," and he closed the door.

The guard yelled orders toward the battlements, which was followed by the grating of the gate, the carriage continuing its journey within. It was not long before the reinsman slapped the reins, the carriage coming to a halt. There was a thud, the familiar click, and the door swinging open. "May you find joy in your stay, my lady," he said, taking her hand as Agustina exited the carriage.

He seems unmoved by the previous fight. Has he had other violent pursuits? He escaped with such ease.

Then, Lionus followed suit, the reinsman abandoning them in the empty streets. The marketplace was silent, the vendors' carts left empty as night had come to find them. There was a flame in the distance, a guard talking with another in a city corner.

Agustina led the way through it. Then, Lionus saw a movement from the corner of his eye. A group of men had turned in their direction and were approaching quickly.

We are being followed. Is it the men from the forest? Or the ones who killed Wilken? Perhaps they are following us because of the gift we escorted. Nay, perhaps they are mere looters intent on robbing us.

Lionus snatched her hand, and Agustina turned to look at him. "Do you hear that?" he asked, taking the lead, preventing her from stopping.

"What?" her voice mimicked his whisper.

"Do not turn, but we are being followed," Lionus tugged her hand. There was a light shiver in her hand, but as his grip tightened, it subsided. For a moment, the footsteps vanished.

Are they gone? Was I mistaken?

But then the footsteps came alive once more. Agustina's hand trembled, and he knew he was not going mad.

She knows as well.

His heart raced, for he knew there were multiple footsteps. *Three. Four perhaps? Are these the men from the forest?*

They became louder with each moment. An alleyway ahead came into view.

That is where we must turn to escape them.

He turned towards it and pulled Agustina behind him, the pair entering. But he realized they were surrounded. Surrounded by walls. It was a blind alley.

Agustina's breathing fastened, and she looked around, as if searching for an escape.

Lionus pivoted to her, Agustina looking up at him. There was a flash in her eyes, and she seized his other hand. His stomach tightened. The steps closed in, each step striking louder than the last. Their voices became audible, and Agustina reached for his chin. Lionus cocked an eyebrow. *What is she doing?*

"Kiss me, Lionus."

"Have you gone mad?" his eyebrows furrowed. Lionus turned away from her, his gaze fixed on the street, hand on his pommel.

The steps became louder, louder, louder. The voices were nearly discernible, and Lionus knew he would need to fight them. He gripped his sword's hilt.

This is it.

The voices were around the corner, tearing through the silence of their ragged breathing.

There was a tug, the gentleness of Agustina's hand reaching for his chin and turning him toward her. She slipped her hand behind his neck and pulled him down. Before he could comprehend what was occurring, they were locked in a kiss, her soft lips upon his, leaving him breathless.

She is mad.

But confusion was stirred in a pot with a sensation he had not sensed in quite some time.

The voices rounded the corner, and shadows were cast upon them. "Ha!" one of the men said. In a slurred speech, he continued, "The lot of you should get a brothel. Stealing our piss spot with your fornication."

Another man behind him laughed.

It does not seem robbing us was their aim after all.

Lionus wrapped an arm around Agustina, pulling her closer. Their bodies met, her softness pressing against his firm frame. With their lips locked, the conversation beside them carried on.

"There be more piss spots 'round here. Let them be," said a third man. There was a scoff, and the men withdrew.

They were abandoned by the men, yet they remained close, their lips grazing, as if what had happened belonged to a world apart from the matter at hand. The familiar scent seemed to wrap Lionus once more. There was a swift inhale from Agustina, and she stopped caressing his hair.

Lionus opened his eyes, only to be met by her lively gaze. *What was that?*

"Forgive me," he reeled back. *Was that an unchivalrous thing to do?* "I should not have kissed you."

"It was not you who kissed me," Agustina shied away while tucking a strand of hair behind her ear. "It was upon my request, to protect me, and my plan proved fruitful. They let us be." Then she looked up at him. "You seem quite tense, Sir Lionus."

Was this the only way? Why would she kiss me, even if to cause them to abandon us? Who would have imagined a kiss would be an honorable way to protect a lady, particularly in a world where sword and shield are the most suitable defense? He let out a sigh. *But even then, it is as if I betrayed Eleni.* But he knew she was gone. It was not an offense. But even after her death, even after the time that had come to pass, a devotion for her still lingered in his heart.

Agustina slid her hand down his neck, then stepped away.

"Aye. I should have found another way to shield you," he averted his gaze.

"It was a strategic survival method. A well-thought-out plan, if I may," she paused. "Your neck is tense, Sir Lionus," she said, "the burdens of our travels have not allowed you to rest."

"Seems not," he grasped his neck. *I am merely uneasy. Perhaps this strategy was what we needed.*

Suddenly, a pair of footsteps began to approach.

One man. Alone. Who is coming for us now?

Lionus looked at Agustina, then stepping before her, he shielded her from the incoming danger. The footsteps tore through the silence, and Lionus unsheathed his sword. Lionus' fingers tingled, and he tightened his grip. Then, a figure carrying a chest lunged around the corner, a shrill cry escaping him. The figure tumbled and fell back, his hood falling from his face.

"Spare me, Sir Lionus," the man said, reaching for the chest which had fallen beside him.

"Who are you?" Lionus pointed the tip of his sword towards the man's chest.

How does he know my name? Who is he?

"The name is Titus, your Monk of the Claw," he said, smiling. "I have pressing information for you," he searched his cloak. Titus pulled out a scroll, the seal of House Valenour upon it.

Lionus snatched the scroll, and it read:

Sir Lionus,

Cretorian Knight accepted into the Hall of the Summoned of the Sanctii Cretorium. You have given your vow to me, Lady Valeciia, and you have sworn to protect that which is dear to us. Once your quest is fulfilled, your final task to enter the Hall of the Chosen lies in this scroll. A Cretorian Knight's loyalty to this family is all that matters. Once you have fulfilled your quest, you must make peace with the past and that which may become dear to you. As your final duty for induction, you must eliminate she who has led you from Accreton to Argentum. May your sword be sharp, and your blood thick.

May your loyalty never falter,
Valeciia Valenour.

"What is the matter?" Agustina asked.

He faced her, his gaze flicking once more to the scroll, then back to Agustina. He felt the blood drain from his face. As if his own fear reflected upon her, he could merely stare at Agustina, for his heart ached under the thought of what must be done.

Honor and loyalty. To who? And at what expense?

CHAPTER 10: THE LION IN THE SKY

After Lionus received the scroll, Titus warned him to fly south, for the Valenours' ships were in danger. He was given a dragon horn, and with it, he summoned Dalax outside Argentum while Agustina remained in the city.

Now, flying southwest, he wondered how far off the ships would be. He leaned forward, holding onto Dalax's reins.

What danger awaits? How will I fight it?

Then, as he flew, he recalled the scroll.

Will I truly slay Agustina? Must I? What threat does Agustina pose that a dagger alone could silence it? Why does Valeciia wish for her death? Does she seek to sever any loose ends?

As Dalax cut through the sky, the first rays of morning rose behind him. The sky had a soft, orange-pinkish hue. Before him, he eased his grip on the dragon's reins and admired the dragon horn he had been granted. Elaborately adorned with the silver leaves of House Valenour, it bore scratches along its surface, now filled with gold-like rivers slicing through it.

How many men have carried this? How many battles has it seen? With all these scratches, it is certainly brimming with history.

A cloud of smoke merged with the clouds. *I did not save the sailors. The shadow of death is all that remains.*

There was a painful lump in his throat. He loosened the reins, and Dalax dove, spearing through a cloud. The world below came into view, lush forests covering the landscape, meeting the rocky shore below. Beyond the shore, he spotted the cloud of smoke which had merged with the sky above. One ship remained, and it was set aflame, listing heavily to the starboard side.

In a matter of moments, he reached the ocean, Dalax's wings scraping against the water below. They made their way toward the ship, Dalax flying past it. A gust of wind blew through the ship, but the flames were inextinguishable. It was nearly completely underwater, and the few men who were alive had leapt into the water.

A few stragglers had managed to pick up the remaining men, lifting them onto a boat they were sailing around the sinking vessel.

How can we be of aid to these men?

As Lionus turned around and began to ascend, the men's screams grew louder.

We are flying farther, and their voices sound louder. They must be yelling at us.

It was then that Dalax peered up, a shadow spearing past them. That is when Lionus understood the shouts. "Dragon!" and their warnings turned to screams. A dragon incinerated the boat below, and Dalax roared as his rival flew past them.

The other dragon was a deep violet-black, as if a starless night refused to loosen its grip upon the coming dawn. It continued flying, heading far toward the shore and rising above the cliffs.

I must not allow it to escape.

"Dalax!" Lionus pulled the reins in the direction of the fleeing dragon.

As he began his pursuit, the dragon started to ascend, going above the cliffs, high into the sky. Finally, it was swallowed by the clouds.

Be careful, Dalax.

Yet the beast flapped its wings and made a swift ascent. Dalax did not compare in size with the other beast, but his speed far surpassed it.

Dalax surged through the clouds and broke above them. The morning that was visible earlier had vanished, and a storm overtook the western area where they were flying. Lightning tore through the sky, and a heavy rain swept across it. Lionus shielded the rains with his hand, his other on the reins.

I must find the dragon. I can scarcely see up here. If I do not find him soon, it will be the end of me.

Momentarily, the sky dimmed, and Lionus looked up, his heart hitching as a shadow flew past. Through the dense rain, it vanished. He shivered, uncertain if he was prepared for what might come.

I have never fought another dragon. How will I kill it? Go for the neck? The wing?

A second shadow rushed past him. Lionus' stomach tightened as he glanced around. Nothing.

We are not alone. He is here.

Then, as if he sensed it, he tightened his grip. From below came a dragon head. Dalax turned to face it, but the beast was upon them. Instinctively, Lionus pulled on the reins. The enemy dragon's teeth scraped Dalax's neck, its claws snatching his wing, Lionus' legs weakening briefly. Dalax roared, spun midair, then released a flame at his opponent.

Lionus held on for his life as he pleaded to the gods, his dragon upside down as the two beasts became tangled in the air. With none able to fly, they spiraled to the world below, scratching, biting, setting each other ablaze. Clouds of smoke formed, and the dew and rain turned to sweat as flames brushed past Lionus. His heart was drumming faster than ever, his hands clenched so tight he believed he would tear through his gloves.

The other dragon bit Dalax's wing, and his beast roared for all Argentum to hear.

"Drage Ignis!" Lionus yelled the ancient Melanoriian command that compelled his dragon to unleash fire. Dalax craned his neck and let out a flame unlike any Lionus had ever seen, Lionus breathless at the sight. The opposing dragon's head burned, and it turned away. Dalax clawed for his life, penetrating his opponent's violet-black wings.

There was a second roar, this time from their opponent. The other dragon released them, and they continued to spiral past the clouds. Lionus pulled on the reins, his hands moist, his grip beginning to slip. He tugged at them, hoping to regain control, but Dalax continued to spiral helplessly. The world below came into view, the cliffs now distant, yet Dalax and Lionus nearing them swiftly.

"Dalax!" Lionus tugged again, and Dalax tucked his wings. They speared through, the beast gaining speed as he approached the water. Lionus' fingers turned cold, and a sour taste overtook his mouth.

This is it. This is it. We are going to hit the water. We are going to meet Malefic.

When they neared the water, Dalax spread his wings wide. He let out a shriek as the water caressed his wings, as if he were seeking it to cure his injuries.

Then, Dalax rose again, beating his wings and escaping the water below. From above, the opposing dragon speared downward. Dalax's eyes narrowed, and he was on a steadfast mission. With the mightier dragon approaching, Dalax hastened, flapping faster, gaining speed and elevation with each moment.

Fly, Dalax, fly!

The beast had the descent in its favor, speed and size aiding it. Lionus was nearly certain his fate was inevitable. He leaned forward and hoped the gods favored him today.

As the two beasts closed the distance, he yelled, "Drage Ignis!"

In the last instant, Dalax hurled a flame at the beast's snout, then spun left. Turning upside down, in the animal's momentary blindness, Dalax clawed at its wings and slapped its neck with his tail. Their opponent slapped them, and Dalax lost control, but he quickly regained it. The other dragon let out a roar.

Lionus glanced back, and their enemy was plummeting. Their opponent fell until he was nearly over the trees. Lionus hooted in triumph, raising his fist into the air as he leveled Dalax. Then, as he glanced back down, the dragon flapped its wings and soared again. Lionus sighed. He stared at the dragon retreating, vanishing beyond the trees, until he was gone.

"We won? We won, Dalax!" he patted the beast's scales. *We won our first dragon battle!*

Dalax, however, let out a roar, and for a moment seemed to glance back.

"Well, you certainly did the fighting," he chuckled, "you saved us." Then, Lionus saw the tear in his wing. "You have suffered a grievous injury. We must tend to your wounds," he caressed Dalax's scales, then embraced him.

Lionus watched the treelines, and seeing no movement, he hoped their opponent would not return. He made his descent to the beach, searching the skies before they landed.

He is gone.

Scattered banners, boats, and men littered the coastline as they flew over, most groaning or dead. Dalax crashed onto the sand, his body sliding until his head met the crashing waves.

Lionus dismounted the beast, searching the coast for survivors.

Did anyone survive? Did we truly not save a soul?

Most had perished, their skins charred from the dragon flames. Others begged for an end to their suffering. He lent one his dagger and continued, searching for anyone who might tell him what had occurred and what the ship's cargo contained.

A man lay on the shore, his hand missing, a metal hook in its stead. He clutched his leg tightly, bone jutting through his hose. Lionus grimaced as he approached him.

The man said, "You came for us, lad. Any other man would have left us to perish after seeing our ship aflame."

"I missed the battle. I did not save you all." Lionus took a knee beside him. *This is what a war with dragons does. Total demise. Total destruction in moments. No man is safe in a land where dragons roam.*

"You came. You could have not come," he said between groans. "That was Ulrin the Unbeatable. You survived a battle with the beast. Many say he is nearly as old as Isabel's dragons. Stolen from the pits!" the man raised his hook, pointing to the sky.

Lionus glanced back, but then the icy touch of the metal hook met his shoulder. "He will not return. I have never heard the beast roar as loud as he did today. You have won a great victory. What is your name, lad?" Then the man looked down at Lionus' hand, staring at the ring. "What may I call you, Sir?"

Lionus hesitated, then shook his head. *Can one call it a victory when so many lives were lost?* "The name is Lionus. And you?"

"Lionus, the Lion in the Sky. You are a hero. I will sing of you when I return home. If I had a second arm, I would play the lute for you! Ha! The name is Magnus the Mad," he cackled, but then shook his head. "Forgive me, lad. These are not festive times, but it is not every day a dragon comes to your rescue."

Lionus looked at his leg, "How are you bearing the pain with such ease?"

The man laughed, "It is the madness." Then he frowned and searched a satchel beside him, pulling a vial from within. "The remedy to all pain," he raised the vial, then took a swig of the violet drink."

Perhaps it is the madness, or perhaps this potion has some unknown magic to us all.

Then, Lionus looked at his ring. Perhaps I can be of aid with it. He put his hand on the man's leg, and a surge of energy rushed through his hand. The man's injury began to improve, and there was a burning pain in his hand unlike any he had ever felt. Lionus faltered, and he braced himself with his hand in the sand. He groaned, then released the man's leg. Lionus panted and looked at the wound, which had barely healed after his touch. Even then, it had weakened him drastically, Lionus attempting to catch his breath.

How could Valeciia heal me with this? How was she able to heal me without nearly dying? I have never been this weak.

The man shook his head, and Lionus grabbed his shoulder, "I will seek help so you may return home."

"You shall not," he leaned forward and seized Lionus arm, "our lady Valeciia spoke of you to us. You have a quest. We have failed you. Her supplies will not arrive in time, but I have sent a messenger to send aid and to warn her of our disastrous expedition.

"It does not matter. All is lost," Lionus slumped on the sand beside him, "less you have a siren to seek the treasures we carried, there is nothing which may be done."

The man replied, but Lionus did not hear his words as he spoke, for he stared beyond the man's shoulder, fixated on the most peculiar sight he had ever spotted.

In the distance, beyond his dragon, what seemed to have been the face of a woman, appeared to be watching. Her hair was as dark as a starless night adorned with shells. Before he could focus, it vanished, a lengthy tail rising before splashing into the water. He touched the base of his neck, and for a moment, he believed he was becoming mad.

Dalax, however, turned in its direction as well. After staring at it for moment, he continued his respite near the water.

Lionus could not contain his stare, and the man snapped him out of his thoughts.

"Hey lad, have you been bewitched? I said siren, and it is as if you have seen one," he cackled. Lionus, without turning, tilted his head sideways. He laughed with the man, but his thoughts remained afar. *Perhaps I did. Perhaps I did.*

CHAPTER 11: A KNIGHT'S MONK

After the dragon battle, Lionus returned to Argentum. He rejoined Titus and Agustina in her manor, where they sat in the study beside the main hall.

I cannot understand why Valeciia wishes for me to kill her?

The study was lined with bookshelves filled with Argentum tomes, maps of Emerion, wax seals, and scrolls littering the hundreds. There was a pelt bear rug before the table, and multiple chairs in the corners.

"Ah, it is great to see you in good health, Master Lionus," Titus said while sitting in a chair beside him. He was a thin, pale young man with sunken eyes, soot-colored straight hair, and a cloak lined in red. His leather boots squeaked with every step, and he had removed his matching gloves and set them on a table beside the books.

"Titus, lad, remind me, what is the purpose for you to be with us Cretorian Knights?" Lionus asked while Agustina stood beside him, cleansing the wound on his neck. *Is he a squire we receive for being a Cretorian Knight?*

"A great inquiry, my good sir," said the young lad with sun-gold eyes. "I am here to aid in any task you require."

"A servant?" he crossed his arms over his chest while observing Titus.

"Not quite," the lad chuckled, "I am here to help you repent of your sins and educate you in our ways." He pointed towards the main hall, "There is much for you to learn. Oh, I nearly forgot, I have your Cretorian armor as well," he said while leaping from his chair.

For an ill-looking lad, he seems in good health.

As the lad left the study, Lionus contemplated his words. *My sins? What must a Cretorian Knight learn?*

Lionus looked at Agustina. She had come around and was now cleansing his face with a cloth. She smiled, glanced in the lad's direction, then shrugged. "He is a decent lad. I believe you will come to like him," Agustina said.

"Repent my sins?" Lionus turned away.

Agustina chuckled while dipping the cloth and wringing it, but Lionus remained still.

Does he speak of my current sins, or the one final murder Valeciia wishes me to commit?

"Aye, Sir Lionus. All of them," Titus said from outside the study, his boots' squeaks growing louder. "Any man or creature you kill, you must repent. It is our way. The Valenours are quite the pious folk." Titus made his way into the study, a tower of books in his hands. "Here we go. The first ones you will need for your lessons."

"The first?" Lionus' jaw fell agape as he stared at the stack of books. *Will I be attending an Emerion university?*

Agustina looked away, kicking his foot lightly.

"Aye, Sir Lionus. There is much to learn."

That is a fair amount of reading. I am a simple man, of a simple family. I have not been taught to read. Symbols and images are the best I can do. Lionus shook his head. "I am certain we can condense this, can we not?" But the boy was halfway out into the main hall, and Lionus was left without a reply.

"A sharp sword requires a golden tongue if it is to survive in court," Agustina said while putting the cloth away. She patted her hands dry, then went to the bookshelf beside Lionus.

Lionus remained silent. *A sharp sword. Is that how Valeciia wishes for me to fulfill my final deed? Or will it be poison? Nay. I cannot do this. Why should I kill Agustina? Is it what the gods have destined for me, or is it simply Valeciia's will? Is it necessary?*

Agustina hummed behind him, and she returned with a book in hand. She sat in the chair beside him. "Do you know how to read?"

Lionus ears burned. He cleared his throat before replying, "I fear the one thing I can read is a liar's expression. Inked pages, however, never came upon them."

"Well, perhaps we may not be able to teach you how to read by the feast, but I am certain we may yet be able to polish your dancing skills," she said as she handed him a book and swung it open. "Illustrated."

"What is the matter with my dancing?" he asked while touching the base of his neck.

Agustina grimaced and looked away, "I fear it is not quite as polished. Not a matter I cannot tend to."

"You bring me to your home, then make a jest out of my dancing skills?" Lionus turned the page to an image of a woman and man dancing. *How am I to kill a woman who is this cheerful and aids me in every way? It is mad, senseless!*

He looked up at her, and as Agustina always was, she was all smiles. "We will make you the envy of the court in a matter of time."

Outside the hall, there was a scraping sound, and Titus returned to the study. He carried a chest, and when he reached the entrance, he unlocked it and brought out a helmet. It was a ruby-crest Cretorian Knight Barbuta helmet. He handed it to Lionus. It had a dent in the visor, as if it had been smashed by a spiked mace. Even then, the damage seemed minor. "We must take it to the smith, but this is your new helmet if you are to represent Lady Valeciia."

"The last knight did not seem to have quite the ending," Lionus gulped. *Is this the end that awaits me?*

"A formidable death for a formidable knight. He died honorably, as all Cretorian Knights should. You have quite the greaves to fill," Titus said while leaning in and emphasizing his final words.

On the visor, there still remained a speck of blood. Lionus took the helmet, and it reeked of iron. He jerked back at the smell. *Needs a proper cleansing.* Lionus then returned it to Titus. "I will have it repaired and cleansed tomorrow, Sir Lionus. It will befit a man of your caliber. I wish we could have had it sooner, yet it took time to locate it from the looters who snatched it."

"Titus, who rides Ulrin the Unbeatable?" Lionus asked while cupping his chin. *If he is this educated, he must certainly know.*

"I fear of all the knowledge I have acquired during my years, I am not quite acquainted with that minor detail," Titus set the helmet in the chest.

How did he even bring all these things to Argentum on his own?

"Then, of the attack, how did they know? How did you find me?"

"Oh, sir. Our web lies deep within Emerion. Knowledge of our plans to forge an alliance with the Argentums has spread. Do not be caught unaware if the Valenour siblings fight over this alliance. The ship carried the supplies required to form our alliance. I fear this may delay our negotiations," he searched within the chest, "but fear not," he brought out a dagger, "we have sent word to Valeciia, and she will find a way to send more supplies. Meanwhile, it is in your hands to bide us time if we are to survive this war."

Lionus leaned back onto the chair. *Great. Negotiations. I believed I was to fight for our people as Cretorian Knights are sworn to do, not serve as an ambassador.*

He must have sighed, because Agustina patted his hand, "Do not fret, Sir Lionus. I will aid you in these negotiations."

If you knew. If you simply knew of my final quest after you have aided me... Oh, Agustina, you would flee until no one had the faintest idea of who you are.

"I am honored. However, how will we manage this when we have nothing to negotiate with?"

Agustina patted his hand and smiled, "Sir Lionus. There is always a way. There is always a way."

CHAPTER 12: NO FAIR PLAY

After being in the study, Lionus, Agustina, and Titus went to the main hall where they had supper. Titus played tunes on his lute, Lionus and Agustina practicing their dancing before they were to go to Argentum's court, Lionus thinking incessantly about Valeciia's final quest.

After practicing and drinking for hours, Lionus had become dizzy, the wine taking its toll on his footing. He tugged Agustina toward him, and they moved deliberately as the tempo of Titus' music decreased. They were meddled in laughter, their warm breaths mingling in the narrow space they shared. For a moment, as they laughed, the effect of the wine made Lionus forget Valeciia's task.

"Tell me, Sir knight, do you tend to visit ladies' homes and attempt to swoon them with your wine footing?" Agustina asked, narrowing her eyes at him.

"Not quite. I simply pretend so it is they who come sweep me off my feet in their lessons," he said, leaning down towards her.

Agustina laughed and released his hand, slapping his chest lightly. "You are terrible, knight. How dare you trick a lady in such manner."

Lionus took her hand where it rested against his chest, "Perhaps I may not be the kindest knight after all."

Agustina pursed her lips, looking at him intently, her hand wrapped by his as he held her close. Beside them, Titus continued to play, but his attention was now directed toward the servants who had come to sit beside him. Agustina's gaze flickered toward them, then she said, "We have yet to learn if that is true." She slid her hand from his grip. "There is something I wish for you to see."

Something for me to see? Lionus offered his arm, and she accepted it with a smile. She led them to the end of the main hall, Lionus and Agustina exiting toward the back of the manor. They soon entered the manor's garden, brimming with roses all around. There was a waterfall in the center with a nobleman statue, as if he were tending the flowers, and a bench before it. In the corner was a tower, and led him towards it. Before reaching it, she plucked a rose and inhaled its sweet aroma. She handed it to Lionus. He took it and cocked an eyebrow, Lionus uncertain of what to do with it. Agustina lowered her head, and he recalled what she had done before they arrived at Argentum. He placed it lightly in her hair, and she smiled, then continued to lead him towards the tower.

She took his hand, and together they climbed the spiral staircase to the top. The tower's roof was broken, and a fourth of its wall was gone. This, however, did not deter Agustina. She held firmly to his hand as she sat along the edge, gently raising her dress to avoid tripping over it. She then patted the spot beside her.

Lionus complied, and Agustina crossed her hand over her lap. *Why did she bring me up here to this broken tower?*

They were silent, and she gazed toward the keep. It was a long, winding path leading to it, and beyond, the keep rose above the entire city. Three spires rose from its northern side, while two walls spread like wings to the east and west. Waterfalls cascaded down the walls into the city below, and the easternmost one appeared to spill into the Silver Sea.

"They say Argentum was founded by the Valenours," Agustina said, looking at the sky, as if a Valenour would swoop down on its dragon. "It is said that all who once lived here bore Melanoriian blood. I find it peculiar, since not all are dragon riders. Yet, the way the city is built, they say its architecture resembles that of the lost city of Valenoriia. Three spires, and these two walls," she pointed towards the waterfall-filled walls, "they are said to resemble the wings of the diamond dragon. Hence, the water. When day comes, the sun's rays reflect in such a manner that it is as if diamonds are embedded upon it. Quite the beauty, do you think not?"

"It is a sight to behold," Lionus leaned forward while staring at the waterfalls.

"Some even state it looks like a dragon from above," she turned to him, "but I have never flown over it to be certain."

"Do you believe it to be true? The reason Valenoriia met its doom?" Lionus asked, his voice softening as he glanced at her.

"I do not know. But if there is one thing I am certain of, it is the grandest love tale ever sung by bards," she said, a twinkle in her eye, as if the stars were reflecting upon it.

"But he was mad, was he not? Or did love make him mad?" Lionus wondered, his eyebrows furrowing. He had heard many tales, many songs about the Fall of Valenoriia, but he was uncertain which could be true. It was an age-old tale, perhaps a legend. None had found the city. *Could it be real?*

"Does love not make us all mad? Does logic not cease to exist when we fall in the clutches of those whom we yearn?" she asked, clutching her chest, as if feeling for her own heart.

"But if logic ceases to exist, how can we be certain we will do what is suitable?" Lionus raised his hands, shrugging.

"If one loves by logic, then one never truly loves as deeply as one can. Logic is a limitation in that realm. When one truly loves, one would do things unimaginable in any circumstance. Do you not believe it? Do you not believe you could do things for those you love that you never thought yourself capable of doing?" she asked, crossing her arms over her chest.

What would I not do, and what would I do for love? I would have done it all to have Eleni by my side. Anything. Everything. Whatever the gods would have asked of me. Yet, our fates have been cast, and I should not question their decisions. I loved her deeply, but if our fates were sealed in such a manner, then there must be a greater purpose behind it. But what? Why? "Perhaps." *Was it their will for me to meet Agustina?*

"You would. I can see it in you, Lionus. I have heard it in your voice. Love and war, they have no rules. Perhaps that is why they are such a dangerous force to behold. Perhaps it is why many fear their clutches."

"Would you go to the depths of Emerion for love? Would you defy duty and loyalty for it?" Lionus inquired, rubbing his chin. He recalled the letter. *Why must I eliminate Agustina? What has she done? Is she a traitor? Perhaps Valeciia thinks she is the one who told our enemies about the ships sailing to Argentum. She could not have. She seems quite honorable. But then, why would Valeciia have her eliminated? I must learn more.*

"To whom do you owe loyalty? Is it not failing your duty and loyalty to your lover if you abandon them? Is it not failing the realm if you choose your lover?" Agustina asked, her attention fixed on the ring on her finger. She remained silent, then removed the ring. "See?" she placed the ring on his hand. "My late husband served our realm and died for it. I accepted his duty, and he served loyally until his last breath. Yet, in the end, I lost him. Did he think of who could protect me when he was gone?"

Lionus held her hands firmly in his. *I cannot imagine how terrible it must have been for her. She knows what I have felt with Eleni. She must have felt a similar sensation.*

Agustina continued, "I bear no ill thoughts against him, but do you understand what I mean? There is no true victory in love and war. All is fair. There is much to be won, but much more to be lost."

"Forgive me, I did not know," Lionus said, pressing his lips.

Agustina simply shook her head. "You are not at fault, Lionus. This was many ages ago, once, when we were young and carefree. I have endured," but even then, her eyes welled, and a tear rolled down her cheek.

"Hey," Lionus raised her chin, then wiped the tear rolling down her cheek. She bit her lower lip, and a lock of hair fell over her face as she held in the tears that appeared to be welling up within her.

"I am not safe in this world. I am exposed to the dangers of the realm, of court, of life, of love," she wiped a second tear before it rolled down her cheek.

"You are safe," he said, taking her hand once more in his. *She protected me. She has been there for me since we met. Regardless of that letter, I am indebted to Agustina for standing steadfast by my side. I must learn Valeciia's true intentions behind this quest. Perhaps there is a way around this.*

"I will keep you safe, Agustina, just as you have cared for me." But in the end, he did not know how he would stay true to his word.

It seems, in love and war, there is no fair play.

CHAPTER 13: THIEF IN THE PALACE

A month had come to pass as they waited for Lord Merleau, the Lord of Argentum, to return to the city. They had remained studying and learning about Argentum while awaiting his arrival. Once they learned he was in the keep and holding a feast, Lionus and Agustina decided to visit him.

"Who is this soldier?" the guard at the palace entrance asked while lowering his spear. "Lower your hood."

Agustina glanced at Lionus, his body wrapped in a charcoal cloak concealing his entire appearance. A mere rose brooch held it together, Lionus glaring at the man.

"This is my personal guard," Agustina said while turning to the guard. "It will not be necessary. You know well that a woman of my house requires to be escorted to events such as these."

The guard frowned while looking down at her brooch, identical to the one holding Lionus' cloak. He looked at Lionus from head to toe, then raised his spear. "May you enjoy the festivities, my lady."

As they entered, a silver chandelier hung from the high-arched ceiling of the great hall. It was brimming with candles, and though it seemed like the centerpiece of the hall, it was not. With each step, Agustina noticed that Lionus' gaze remained fixed on the far end of the hall. Every time she entered, Argentum's great hall stole her breath away, Agustina covering her mouth with her hand. Five steps led up to the wide dais, at the corner of the base, a pair of silver stags standing erect, commanding the crowd's presence. But their presence was not as commanding as the stag-horned throne that sat at the center of the dais. It was adorned with smoky furs, as if it were a victim of what lay behind it. Beyond it, it was unlike any entrance, a passageway resembling a dragon's snout agape, the torches within it mimicking the flame building within a dragon before it releases its fury into the world. The wall that rose above the dragon's mouth was made of glass, reflecting the great hall's ceiling and the crowd gathered within, the chandelier in its center. Parallel to the cascade-like glass, a pair of ebony banners with a silver stag each, hung, glimmering, as if recently raised for the current festivities.

Agustina, however, knew this not to be true. Whenever she frequented, the banners were always in a similar state. *Argentum's keep is always immaculate.*

"I would have never imagined this place to be like this," Lionus said, pointing towards the far end of the hall.

"Stunning? Magnificent? Glorious?" Agustina asked, her lips slightly parted as she looked at him. *This is a hall like no other. Does it truly resemble Valenoriia? If it does, was Valenoriia supposed to be even more magnificent then?*

"Like the stories," Lionus said, facing her. There was something in his gaze that caused her stomach to flip. Something she had not felt for months, years. Perhaps, only once in her life.

"Of Valenoriia?"

"Of Argentum," he said, crossing his arms over his chest while admiring the hall, "I never imagined to visit this land. The mountains and sea seemed like a hindrance to my exploration, and yet, here I am."

There was a wonder in his eyes, yet even then, there seemed to be an evident gloominess. It had been there since she had met him. For a moment, she hoped it would vanish, yet it lingered still, though waning with time.

"Lady Agustina," a beady-eyed man wearing a wine-colored surcoat joined them.

"Lord Gervais," she gasped, "I did not believe you would return so soon. I prayed for your safety once we left Alzeriia. It gladdens me to see you standing, alive and whole. How did you survive?"

"Oh, my lady," he said while placing a hand on his chest, "we ambassadors have a way of surviving unlike any other man. I would say my own survival weighed least upon me. Have you heard the tales?"

"What tales?" Agustina leaned closer, as though they shared some quiet secret. Even then, their voices were nearly inaudible to each other, for the clamor of the great hall and the minstrel's music served as a veil to their world of secrecy.

"I have come upon hearsay of troops being camped around six days' march from Argentum," Gervais closed the gap between them.

A chill crept through her limbs, and she pressed her fingers to her lips. "Who has troops in such proximity to Argentum?"

"I fear our reports are limited. Why they are coming? That is the matter of importance," Gervais glanced over his shoulder. "We have no quarrel with our neighbors."

"Perhaps they are moving elsewhere," she looked up at the ceiling, praying to the gods they would not come to Argentum.

"I do pray it is so, my lady. I do not wish for our land to be soiled in blood. Many brave men have been lost in wars past," he said, taking a light bow. It was nearly imperceptible, but Agustina's years of friendship with him allowed her to perceive it. He knew how she had been torn after the passing of her husband, how those days had caused such a deep ache in her heart. "Will you be speaking with Lord Merleau this evening?"

"As should be done in all festivities," Agustina winked.

"He is fond of you," Gervais pointed in the direction of the lord who was descending the stairs from the dais.

"My father's loyalty to him has aided in cultivating our bond throughout the years," she smiled.

Gervais nodded, "Your papa's loyalty is unmatched. Send him my regards. I will send Lord Merleau your way."

She was going to refuse him, but before she could speak, he had become one with the crowd and slithered away towards their dear lord.

"Where is Titus?" Lionus whispered, his cloak brushing against her arm. A bolt rushed up to her shoulder, the hairs on her nape rising. She remained silent as she composed herself. *What is the matter with me? This is not who I am. No one causes this in me, not since…*

Then she answered without looking at him. "He is well on his way. I saw him sneak past the guards once we entered."

"Do you truly believe he will not be captured?"

"I pray he does not," Agustina bit her lip, "do you believe he will?"

What if he is captured? What if he cannot find the cure to heal Dalax's wounds? Dalax has not recuperated as we hoped, and he truly needs it. Enigma, guide him down the right path. He must not be captured.

Lionus shook his head, then faced her. She leaned towards him, as if they were on the verge of sharing a deeper secret than the plot at hand. "It matters little what I believe," he said in his usual solemn tone. Even in their tranquility, his words were filled with strength and peace, as if they could calm any army on the verge of an incoming enemy wave. "It will not change the outcome. Now we must wait, and hope he recovers the cure the lord of Argentum has in his keep."

"Recovers is a kind word for it," Agustina said, pursing her lips and raising her eyebrows playfully.

"Any other word may seem, inadequate," he said, his gaze flickering towards the figure approaching them, "particularly when the Lord himself is on the verge of joining us."

Steal. That is the correct term. But is it truly a sin when it serves a grander purpose? A purpose which, after all, may benefit the lord himself? The cure will not merely aid Dalax, it might very well save Argentum from certain doom.

"Lord Merleau," she said, adjusting her cloak as the sleek, steel-haired man with a rough beard approached them. He wore a surcoat with the colors of his banner, the white stag on his chest glimmering.

"Lady Agustina. Do you ever miss my festivities?" he asked, smiling as he joined them.

"Not for the world," she raised her hand, the lord planting a kiss upon it. He was around thirty years her senior, and his rugged face contrasted with the warm smile he flashed her. He looked at Lionus, the lord of Argentum more robust than the knight beside her. Even now, she was certain he was a formidable warrior, though she had never seen him raise his sword, for it seemed his voice carried more weight than any steel could.

"A new guard, I see," Merleau said, eyeing Lionus curiously.

Merleau is not always quite welcoming of foreigners, but I am certain he will not protest about having a Cretorian Knight in his keep. "From a land far away, yet not quite unfamiliar to ours. This is Sir Lionus." Lionus shook Merleau's hand.

Merleau paused, then nodded, "We welcome visitors, so long as they bring no quarrel in their wake."

"I would not come to think about it," Lionus shook his head.

"I would certainly hope not," he looked him straight in the eye, eyes dark as his banners, yet calmness imbued within them. "Matters to attend in these festive times are many, but time is but a grain of sand per each guest I must share. There are but nine rings in this world, and I seldom behold one in Argentum. Pray tell, your visit is not for pleasure."

She crossed her hands behind her back. *Merleau. Never been one to miss a detail in the world. No pleasantries today with him.* "We have been sent from the forger of the nine rings' daughter."

"My dear, ever bound to that world, even now," Merleau placed a hand on her shoulder, his eyes softening. "I cannot be one to place blame. Our blood runs thick with them. History cannot be altered." He rubbed her shoulder, then took a step back as he shifted his attention to Lionus. "Tell me, Lionus. What does your lady require of me?"

Lionus nodded. "Lord. My lady requests simple resources. Lumber and grain to fund our war and troops. Fire has reigned upon our land, and much has been lost."

"The tales have reached far east. A war of dragons. A broken family. It is a perilous place to be," he took a pause while his gaze shifted between them, as if contemplating what was to come next. "My people will not risk our resources without due recompense."

"Indeed. My lady has stated she will pay adequately for your resources. Precious metals will be sent in return," Lionus leaned forward, as if keeping the exchange between them so no other soul could eavesdrop.

Merleau's eyes widened.

Agustina was breathless. *Melanoriian steel. The strongest steel in the world, originated long before the Fall of Valenoriia. Will she truly send that this way? Or simply other precious gems?*

"Well, I hope she has sent another ship. Last I heard, her ships sank near the southwestern coast of the Silverlands. Not good business if those were the ones carrying her resources," he lowered his voice.

"Your resources will arrive," Lionus said, his voice firm, his semblance not conceding to what seemed like an evident loss.

"I am grateful for your lady's offer," he nodded, "however, we have received a rival offer. No supplies have yet arrived, but given that you have travelled here to meet me, I will accept whichever offer reaches Argentum first. Is that reasonable?"

Agustina's throat became dry, and she gulped. *Who is the other person? Who would strike out a similar deal? Is it the other Valenours? Have they come to undermine us?*

"It is appropriate," Lionus said before she could discuss it with him. Agustina bit her lip, Lionus' gaze flicking to her before refocusing on Merleau. Lionus and Merleau shook on their accord, and Merleau kissed Agustina's hand before departing.

"What have you done?" Agustina snatched his forearm. The touch of it was cold, the metal under his cloak concealing his warm skin. "Are you even aware who this other person might be?"

Lionus took her hand, and even under the touch of his gauntlet, there was a sense of gentleness to it. "Do not fret, Agustina. The matter at hand will be under control. Now, I must make certain Titus does not pit us into any trouble. Will you be well without me?"

Agustina sighed. "Certainly, when have I not been?" she rolled her eyes while shaking her head gently. "I merely brought you along for being an imposing presence," she teased.

Lionus smirked, and without a word, seeped into the crowd.

Agustina was left alone amidst the crowd. *Where is he going? Will he attempt to go beyond the great hall? I should not have allowed him to leave. He knows little of this castle, if anything at all. What if he is captured as well? What will Merleau think of us? No. Lionus is aware of his actions. He is a careful soul. I must simply wait until he returns. All will be well. All will be well.*

Agustina set her thoughts aside and spoke with ladies of the region, and with a few couples of lands far beyond the Silverlands. Many, she seldom saw, yet many more she saw often, by reason of their nearness. Politics, fashion, and the common trivialities of court and beyond were discussed. Agustina enjoyed such festivities, and the friendly nature of the Silverlands and its people always allowed her to indulge in such.

But not all in the Silverlands were of the Silverlands.

"Thief!" A man yelled, and the crowd dispersed.

All Argentums glanced around, searching for the culprit being blamed for such a sin. Suddenly, a figure crashed against her. *Titus?*

Her hands became clammy. *No. They caught you. What have you done?*

Titus slipped his hand behind her cloak. As he watched the crowd, he handed her a bottle swiftly. And just as he appeared, he snaked through the crowd and was gone.

Agustina pinned the bottle against her ribs, glancing around nervously.

The crowd dispersed, men walking in her direction. They were armored, and one brawny figure in burgundy brigandine armor towered over the rest. Just when she believed he would go past her, he pointed at Agustina. Her limbs froze, as if winter had come for her.

He raised his visor, "Thief!" and she saw the strikingly familiar strawberry tongue. The ashy skin of the Muunelviel elves gave way to the elf before her. Most were slender, but he, he was unlike all of them. *Ardrien!* He was the most feared Muunelviel and one of the grandest elven warriors in all the Silverlands. Adrien also happened to abhor Agustina's family for reasons unbeknownst to her.

"I am no thief," Agustina replied while meeting his gaze. She hid her hand under her cloak, hoping he would not see her trembling.

"A thief *and* a liar. Our lord will have your hand and your tongue. I saw the thief hand you a bottle, and I have seen you shelter him in your manor," he said. Ardrien snarled. "Now you dare steal from our lord and spill lies about it." He reached for her, but she sprang back. She collided with a noblewoman, stalling her escape.

"Lay a hand on me and…" she said, glaring at him, but he interrupted her.

"And what? Your friends are gone. You cannot fight. No guard can save you. The truth lies under that cloak. That which you have stolen," Ardrien stepped forward, the two a foot away.

Titus. Lionus. Where are you? Have you two abandoned me?

Lord Merleau had made his way down. "Have you proof of this?"

He has none. Who will he bring to bear witness to Titus being at my home?

"The evidence lies beneath her cloak. Have her reveal it to you," Ardrien pointed at Agustina.

No. I cannot. If I raise it, I die. I am guilty. Titus gave it to me. This is it. There is one way out.

Her heart raced. "I invoke a trial by combat!" she said before she could contemplate the situation further.

Merleau's eyes widened, his skin going pallid. She knew he had no choice in his next action, and he asked Ardrien, "Do you accept?"

Ardrien's gaze narrowed upon Agustina. "Ha, a jest. No one will stand to save you against me," Ardrien turned to the crowd, and his voice boomed, "will any of you come to save her?"

There was silence. The crowd did not move except to whisper to their partners. The minstrel's music had faded beyond the portals of Malefic.

Titus? Lionus? Where are you?

But neither appeared. She searched the hall for them, the world becoming hazy with each passing moment.

"I will fight you myself, if need be, Ardrien," she said, clenching her fist.

"Ha," Ardrien whirled to face Agustina, now inches away from her. "You will meet death with my hand about your throat."

The crowd's silence weighed upon Agustina. Her temples throbbed. *Will I really fight him? I will do it if need be. Ardrien is not wrong. I will meet a merciless death. He is one of the greatest Muunelviel knights in the Silverlands.*

Ardrien smiled at her, snatching her wrist, but Agustina twisted from his grasp.

Then there was a distant gasp. Murmurs erupted. The crowd dispersed.

Clink.

Clink.

Clink.

A familiar rattling resonated through the vastness of the great hall, as if it were soulless, barren. Footsteps, like those of a giant, made their way toward them. The crowd was in awe at the sight; some even trembled.

Agustina searched amongst the crowd, then, she saw it, and gasped.

All knew the ruby crest, the familiar barbuta helmet. There was a glimmer from under the cloak of the knight approaching, but even then, it appeared to swallow all light. The figure's steps were slow, yet each one grew louder. Then it came to a halt, towering beside Agustina.

She sighed, her body weakening.

The crested knight stared at Ardrien. The knight unclasped the rose brooch, the cloak slumping to the ground, only to reveal the Melanoriian steel-plated armor. A ruby cape now took the place of the cloak, clasped by a pair of ironclaw brooches. The center of the steel plate armor bore a dragon egg with a ring on the center scale, a dragon egg held tightly by a pair of iron claws, one with four toes, the other with five, one for each of the Cretorian Knights. The entire crowd gathered in silence.

"Ha," Ardrien said as he took a step back and reached for his sword's grip. "A Cretorian Knight. Pity. You would risk your honor and life for a thief." Ardrien unsheathed his sword.

Lionus unsheathed his own, staring at the elf before him.

Ardrien slapped his visor closed.

There was silence.

Lionus then took a step forward, wrapping his arm around Agustina and pushing her gently behind him.

A shudder escaped her.

Lionus unclasped his cape. Then, staring at Ardrien, he said, "Pity. Now, I will have to crush your skull."

CHAPTER 14: SILENT SILVER HALL

Clang!

Lionus' and Ardrien's swords met, their faces mere inches from each other. They pushed away, and Lionus raised his shield. *I will be the last soul Ardrien sets eyes upon.*

"You believed this would be a simple feat," Ardrien said, his voice slightly muffled behind his visor.

"All warriors deserve a formidable death. I wanted your legacy to be worthy of your words," Lionus said. *These cursed Muunelviel deserve the sword.*

Ardrien roared, and he charged at Lionus.

Lionus waited for him. When he reached him, he sidestepped. Then, he turned to bash his back with his shield. But Ardrien had already turned. As Lionus thrust his shield toward him, Ardrien spun, then bashed Lionus with his own shield. Lionus reeled and shook his head, the world spinning.

"Malefic will curse you all," Ardrien shouted. He swung down at him, but Lionus parried his blow.

Lionus leaned in as their swords crashed, "The flower girl strikes a stronger blow than you."

Ardrien growled and kicked Lionus.

Bang!

He struck his shield, and Lionus' body shook with his force.

"Arrogant knights are the ones who die the swiftest," Ardrien hacked downward at Lionus' head, slicing the tip of his crest as Lionus ducked.

Ardrien slashed down and Lionus parried with his shield. Lionus thrust his sword at Ardrien's abdomen. Ardrien wheeled around Lionus' back, then slashed at him. Lionus swiveled, but Ardrien struck his arm. Lionus stepped back and glanced at where Ardrien slashed him. *Uninjured. This explains why Cretorian Knights survive these battles.*

"Ha! If that is so, it is a surprise you have lived this long. Dull elf with a dull blade," Lionus twirled his sword, "is that why they keep you hidden in castles?"

"Ah! You insolent human!" Ardrien's fury burned with each word he spat. He charged again, Lionus parrying his strike with his shield. Ardrien roared as his sword flew away, yet he continued his charge.

Clang!

Ardrien's pauldron struck the center of Lionus' chestplate, sending him on his back. Lionus lost grip of his sword. *Just what I needed. But he is upset. He will not be fighting as he once was.*

The elf retreated to retrieve his sword. Lionus, however, caught hold of his leg and yanked it. The elf stumbled and struck his face on the ground.

"Ah! You dirty Cretorian." Ardrien missed his sword's grip. He rolled onto his back and drove a kick to Lionus' face. Lionus blocked it with his shield, the elf groaning.

Lionus jumped to his feet, but before he could grab his sword, the elf was up and had seized a shield from a guard. He snatched his sword, and Lionus was left with nothing but his shield. *Cursed be Malefic.* Lionus unsheathed his throwing knife.

Ardrien laughed. "One dagger cannot save you."

The words burned through his memory, reminding him of the night he lost Eleni… of the elf who attacked him and told him those exact words. There was a pain in his jaw, Lionus grinding his teeth as he recalled the horrendous night.

Bang!

Ardrien struck Lionus' helmet with his pommel, leaving him wobbling from the attack. He stumbled backward, clutching his head as the guests seemed to whirl about. The elf attacked again, sending another downward strike.

Lionus focused on him, and his eyes burned, the armor light under his fury. Lionus' heart banged against his steel chestplate. He blocked the downward strike with his shield, but Ardrien was swift to bang him with his own shield. A jolt of pain tensed Lionus' right shoulder. Their shields locked; Ardrien tugged fiercely, seeking to wrench it free and leave Lionus with nothing but his dagger.

Now they were face to face, and Ardrien said, "With your pitiful skills, your family would hang their heads in shame."

In that moment, it was as though a dragon had kindled a fire within Lionus' armor. Heat emanated from his body, and sweat stung his eyes. Lionus forgot all about the world, and he furrowed his eyebrows, the world around him becoming a haze.

Lionus banged his shield against Ardrien's chest, then sent an upward slash to his chin. The elf stumbled, regained his footing, and prepared to retaliate. Lionus, however, was already on him.

You will meet Malefic now!

With a second strike, Lionus disarmed him, his sword crashing on the floor. He slammed his body against the elf, then leapt upon him on the ground.

The elf punched him, but Lionus blocked it with his forearm.

Lionus jabbed his dagger into his armpit, the elf screaming. He pinned Ardrien's sword arm to the ground and bashed his face with his shield.

Bang!

The visor's hinge crushed inward.

Bang!

The visor dented.

Bang!

The helmet flew from his face.

Bang! Crack! Squelch.

The sounds repeated.

Bang! Crack! Squelch!

Murmurs erupted in the hall. Then shrieks. Nobles turned away. Men covered women's eyes. But Lionus. He saw nothing.

Fog. Fog. Fog.

Squelch! Crack! Bang!

All he could hear were Eleni's whimpers. Her last breaths. Her kind heart.

"It is over!" A woman's voice tore through the great hall. Someone grasped his pauldron. He swiveled, ready to decimate his next foe with his shield.

But as he faced her, he beheld her kind eyes. Almond eyes, once sweet, now brimming with fear.

Agustina.

She looked straight at him, her gaze softening. It was as if she could see through his visor. Agustina held both sides of his helmet, her gaze unwavering. "It is over. You defended my honor."

His chest rose and fell. His heart banged, just as he had banged Ardrien's helmet. Lionus took a deep breath, then turned toward the elf.

Except there was no elf. There was an armor, and a squelched mixture of what appeared to be bone with flesh in a soup of blood. The ground stained. The deed done. Looking down, he saw his gauntlets and shield. All filled with blood.

The deed is done. He paused, then sighed.

He stared at what remained, took his dagger, and rose. With that, he grabbed his sword and sheathed it. Lionus walked a couple paces forward, snatched his opponent's helmet, and stared at it.

No more.

He seized the silver-golden helmet by its metal plumes and advanced toward Agustina. By now, she was standing, still staring at him, as if she wished she could undo the damage she had caused this night, a pained expression on her face, Agustina placing her hand on her chest.

Lionus stopped before her. He closed his eyes briefly, then opened them. He gazed down. "It is done. You are safe."

And with that, the once festive Silver Hall fell silent. Lionus walked past her and exited the keep, leaving the floors stained with what he would forever call justice.

CHAPTER 15: SELFISH LOVE

Lionus sat by the edge of the dock, watching the water reflect the moon. He dipped his hands within it, the water biting through the gauntlets and into his skin as it swallowed the blood which stained them. The moon's reflection mixed with the blood, swirling while he moved his hands until he removed them from the water. He stared, and the blood faded, the moon shining clear once more.

The water was calm, and there was a familiar tranquility in the Silver Sea which he had not experienced in a long time. He closed his eyes and inhaled deeply, the subtle smell of salt and damp driftwood dominating the docks. The only sounds came from distant sailors unloading or drinking in the far end of the dock, but even then, it did not suffice to disturb his peace.

He opened his eyes, and as he stared at the water's reflection, a woman came into view. Though he never heard her footsteps, he hoped that now that the trial by combat had concluded, she would only bring peace.

Peace. A costly treasure in this world, and at times, rare to find.

"It is quite the spot, is it not?" Agustina asked as she sat beside him, raising her dress to avoid stepping on it as she sat on the edge of the dock.

"Tranquility at its finest," Lionus said while holding her arm as she made her descent beside him. *It feels like the night we sat at the tower.*

"Quite the contrary to that great hall," Agustina looked at him. Lionus glanced at her, then down at his lap as he removed his gauntlets. They sat there in silence. Agustina watched him struggling to remove the gauntlets, and she closed in to assist him.

"You will stain your dress if it seeps blood," Lionus pulled away, but Agustina held on to his gauntlet.

Agustina looked at him from under her brow, "After all the blood you have spilt for me, the least I can be bothered is by a splotch of blood staining my dress."

Lionus met her gaze, and she flashed him a soft smile. *All the blood I spilt. The elf I killed. Was it necessary? Aye. Must it have been as bloody as it was? Perhaps not.* He bit his cheek. *The past cannot be undone.*

"Perhaps I should not have massacred Ardrien in such a horrific manner. There are nobler ways to die. I do not know what came upon me. It was as if I was possessed by one of Malefic's creatures," he said as she removed his gauntlets. His knuckles were bruised and scratched. Her soft hands met his, Agustina filling the gauntlet with water and letting it run down his hands, cleansing the now dried blood.

"You were not the Lionus I believed I knew," she said, then paused.

She must imagine me to be a murderer, a vicious man.

He was about to reply when she continued, "Yet no man has guarded my honor so nobly. I should never have placed you in such a position. That was selfish of me," Agustina said, wiping the last of the dried blood from his hands.

Lionus flinched, but he gave in to the pain of her caring hands. *Was it selfish of me to kill Ardrien for a crime we truly committed so Agustina could live? Or should I have abandoned her to the fate of the gods? I could not have. She did not deserve to die for a plan we all worked on. She has cared for me, and in our time together, my heart has grown fond of her. I could not let her die. She does not deserve to die… after all…* "Is love not selfish?"

Agustina glanced up at him, her cheeks reddened.

Lionus then added, "Forgive me. I did not mean it in such a way. I meant to say, is caring for those around us not a way of showing love, and we would do anything to care for them?" Lionus glanced away, raking his fingers through his hair. *What am I saying? So much for Lionus the silver-tongued. All in Argentum is silver except the words leaving my lips.*

"You thought you were protecting *her* when you protected me, were you not?" Agustina asked, her hand still over his.

"Aye. No! I thought of her, but merely because of the words he said. Words another elf said the night they took her life. The whole time, however, I saved you for you, not her. I stood up to save you because I care for you. You have been... kind to me."

"Kind?" Agustina said in a solemn voice. Then she repeated it, "Kind?" in a teasing tone. "Lionus, it is no sin if you still think of her. She was your wife. She loved you, and you loved her.

Why is she like this? Lionus could not help but look at her, "Why do you bathe me with such kindness?"

Agustina smiled, slid her arm around his, and leaned against his shoulder, "We can all care for others. Some of us protect the flesh with our swords, others care for the soul with our words."

It seems we are all defenders of the world. "Now, is it not morally wicked if I protected you for being condemned for stealing?"

"But I did not steal," Agustina said. "The bottle Titus gave me was merely water. It was not the true potion. Besides, do I have the hands of a thief?"

Water? Ardrien, in truth, accused her of stealing water. Lionus chuckled. "You do not."

"But I do," Titus said as he crept up behind them.

"Titus," they said in unison, glancing back to cast him a frown.

"Forgive me, sir, lady. Yet, it seems, none of us are truly thieves," he said, clutching his satchel close to his body, his sickly-looking skin mimicking the moon without its glow.

"How is that?" Lionus asked, tilting his body toward Titus as he awaited an answer.

"I *may* have lost the potion," he said, scratching his neck.

The chaos we caused served no purpose. "Cursed be Malefic," Lionus said, but Agustina squeezed his arm. Her touch had a way of calming him in a similar manner to the Silver Sea.

"Do not fret, friends. Lionus, I am here to absolve you of any sins you may have committed on my behalf... or not on my behalf. Cretorian Knights walk a thin line between what must be done and what should be done. That is where I come to snatch your soul from the fiery portals of Malefic's world," Titus said while flashing him a smile, though not as beautiful as Agustina's, for a few teeth were cracked.

"Lovely," Lionus rolled his eyes and turned back toward the sea.

"There is, nevertheless, a way to find another potion. A particular place, quite close to our location," he said, then smiled smugly.

"I feel there is something you are withholding." *This smells like trouble, but what part of this venture has not reeked of trouble this far?*

Titus chuckled, and Lionus braced himself. "Well, you might not be quite fond of who we receive it from, given recent events."

CHAPTER 16: RELIVING MEMORIES

Lionus, Titus, and Agustina made their way towards a ship in Argentum's dock, the pair standing and waiting for its sailors to come ashore.

"Of all the places you could have found one, this was our finest choice?" Lionus asked, staring at the ship, its sailors heading down to the dock.

"Our first quest was of no avail. This is all that remains. For our dear friend to heal, it must be done," Titus said, stretching his neck as he nudged Lionus forward.

From the ship, a trio of Muunelviel men descended onto the dock in cottes, the middle one clad in a grey jerkin. Their pointed ears escaped through the side of their coifs, and they made their way toward them with their glowing eyes in the middle of the night.

"The name is Jack, Jack Muunee," the middle elf said.

"Never heard an elf called Jack," Lionus said, his hand on his pommel. *We finish one Muunelviel, simply to deal with another. Malefic is set against me.*

Jack glanced at Lionus' hand, but he remained calm. "Well, now you know one. Heard you require my services. A particular remedy for your ailments."

"Do you have it?" Lionus narrowed his eyes.

"Would I offer that which I do not have?" he pulled out a silver coin and fiddled with it.

"I do not know you, Jack. Perhaps you do. Perhaps you do not."

This cursed Muunelviel. I do not want to deal with these elves. What have you done, Titus? He will seize all my coin if he is allowed. "What is the cost?" He folded his arms across his chest.

"It is priceless. Would not even gift it," Jack continued, "yet, for a friend," and he grinned knowingly.

"See, we are friends," Titus chipped in, nodding. He flicked his gaze between Lionus and Jack.

"We are not friends," Lionus stared at Jack.

"Ha! But we can be. And we will be. Come now, lad, it is but a simple accord. You do not even know what I wish to have in return," he leaned in as if he were about to tell him a secret.

"Silver? Is that not what you all desire?" Lionus shook his head.

"'Course not, lad," Jack said.

What could he want besides silver?

"Listen to him," Agustina whispered, her hand wrapped around Lionus' arm.

Jack glanced at her, his pointed ear turning in her direction. Lionus took a half step forward.

Jack smirked, "Hearsay has it you are a formidable knight without a retinue. Keep one of my boys as your squire. Educate him in your ways."

"I could never."

A Muunelviel slew my mother, and now he would have me train his boy. Is he mad? It is one thing to strike a bargain with one, quite another to train one and keep him by my side.

"'Course you could, lad," Jack said, winking.

Educate one of these arrogant elves. It is the least that I need.

"We need this," Titus whispered.

Jack smiled, his ears turning to the left where Titus stood on Lionus' opposite flank.

"Name another price," Lionus stepped back. *I will not have a Muunelviel as a squire.*

"A dragon egg, but I am certain you do not have one," Jack crossed his arms over his chest.

Arrogant elf. There is truly no other path. I pray I do not come to regret this decision. In the end, I do require a squire. May the gods watch over me. "Show me the potion."

Jack nodded, and one of his men brought it out. Lionus pointed at Titus, and he advanced forward. After analyzing it, Titus said,

"It is the one."

This is it then. Lionus sighed. "I will do it, but in time, I will require something from the Mathielie Moonlands, as payment for keeping him under my watch. It is a thing most particular to your lands. When the hour comes, will you be able to procure it?"

Jack narrowed his eyes. "Few things are beyond my grasp." Then he smiled, "But I will require a transportation fee, if it is a sizeable object... or beast..."

Muunees. "So long as the price is modest."

"Are they not all?" Jack licked his lips.

Lionus nodded. "Take the potion, Titus. Bring the boy."

The group left the city of Argentum and arrived at Agustina's estate in Val Rozea, slightly south of Zan Rosea, where Dalax had landed when they arrived in the Silverlands. It was flanked by lush forests to its west, a river bordered its south, and fields were strewn out east of it.

Upon their arrival, the sun had set, and Agustina led them to the war room within her estate. An arched entrance granted access into it, the entryway flanked by a pair of bookcases. Uneven stones were laid on the ground, and as they descended the three stairs, a rectangular table with a giant map of the Silverlands was stretched upon it. At the far end, a map of all Emerion hung on the wall, flanked by the silver banners with the bright red rose of House Rozea. To the right, a fireplace stood, a statue of a knight kneeling beside it. Aside from this, there were multiple plants, and though not dust-filled, Lionus imagined the war room was seldom utilized.

Was this war room used in the ancient battles of Argentum? Or did it simply serve a more decorative purpose? Perhaps it served for preparations in minor skirmishes when quelling rebellions.

"Titus, take our squire and see that he aids you in repairing my armor and tending to Dalax," Lionus pointed towards the hall where they had come from.

The young lad was of typical Muunelviel features: the ashy skin, strawberry tongue, glowing eyes. Nevertheless, he was unlike Ardrien, for he was slender yet muscular.

Titus and the lad left, leaving Agustina and Lionus in the war room. She moved a couple of candles from the table. Before she could finish, footsteps rushed into the chamber.

A young girl, around nine winters, rushed in. She wrapped her arms around Agustina, "You are back!" Then, she noticed Lionus, and she stepped back. She fixed her hair and stood straight, preening her dress while she nudged Agustina. "You brought a boy home. And he bears the look of summer. Of Emeros, most certainly."

"You have merely met this knight," Agustina said, shaking her head while looking down at the young girl who was a mirror image of her.

The young girl smiled smugly, placing a hand on her hip. "Do not fret, Agustina. I will not steal his heart. The stable boy is the one pining after my own. Perhaps I will be of sturdy heart. He cannot believe me to be swooning over him so swiftly."

"But you are, dear child," Agustina said, "you are a lover girl at heart."

A lover girl? At such a tender age? She is a humorous little lady.

The young girl gave a cheeky smile and hid her hands behind her back, "I know, but he does not need to know such particulars."

"You are terrible," Agustina said, "forgive me. This is my tenderhearted sister, Rozea."

"Like the estate," Rozea said, beaming and taking a step forward, "Papa named it after me."

"He did not," Agustina said while taking the wooden figurines from a shelf and placing them on the war room table.

Rozea glanced over her shoulder, "There is no need to be jealous, sister. The gods frown upon it."

Agustina rolled her eyes and pushed her gently towards Lionus. "Greet the knight. He is our guest."

Rozea curtsied him, then bowed and raised a hand, "Take a knee, Sir Knight."

"Rozea!" Agustina scolded her.

Rozea giggled, "A kiss will suffice."

Lionus held in a laugh, then followed suit, took her hand, and planted a gentle kiss, "A pleasure to make your acquaintance, my lady."

Rozea blushed and glanced at her sister, "You certainly found a fine one."

"Shush, Rozea! Go fetch papa."

"I am no hound," a voice came from the great hall, "I do not require fetching. I am coming." Through the entrance, a man with straight, chestnut hair, full cheeks, and fair, aged skin came in. He had a clean-shaven face, and his bright eyes were of identical color to his daughters.

"Papa, this is Sir Lionus. Lionus, this is Papa Guido," Agustina said.

"A pleasure, My Lord," Lionus said, bowing lightly as the man entered the war room.

"Oh, call me Guido, Cretorian Knight." *How does he know of my standing?* "If you wonder how I know, news travels fast in these parts. I am grateful for the aid you have given my daughter. Our honor and word are all we possess in this world. Safekeeping it is of utmost importance."

"I would not hesitate to repeat the deed," Lionus said, yet a knot formed in his stomach.

How am I to follow Valecia's orders? How am I to kill Agustina? I see no reason for it. To leave Guido without a daughter. To leave Rozea without her older sister. The mere thought of it torments my soul.

"I would not be one to distrust your word," she said, moving closer. She squeezed his forearm gently while gazing up at him.

The door creaked, and soft murmurs drifted in from beyond the war room. The group became silent, and Lionus listened intently. Guido smiled as the voices drew near. Through the arched entrance appeared a servant, and she stepped aside to allow the ambassador to join them.

"Gervais," Guido said while raising his hands. "My old friend! Welcome! You are tardy."

As they greeted each other, the servant handed a sealed scroll to Rozea. She rushed and brought it to Lionus. The familiar dragon sigil was embedded on the stamp. *Valenour stamp.* The hairs on his nape and arms rose.

Lionus opened it, and it read:

Sir Lionus,

A pair of caravans will be carrying the supplies to Argentum. Both departed from the west but will have a delayed arrival. The one travelling closer to the sea is not the envoy. Burn upon receipt.

Valeciia Valenour

Word has reached Valeciia, and she has sent the resources for our diplomatic mission. No one must learn of this, or we risk being intercepted once more.

Lionus curled it in his fist as Guido said, "I will leave the three of you to it. Plans are to be made. Come, my dear girl."

"But Papa," Rozea cried while stomping the floor.

"Come, do not meddle in matters of grown folk," and he took her away. "Pouting will merely make the stable boy dislike you."

"How do you know about the stable boy?" she asked, Rozea's jaw dropping as her father took her hand.

"Everyone knows, my dear child," and their voices faded in the distance.

Lionus, Agustina, and Gervais then sat around the war room. Gervais discussed the movements of the army approaching Argentum and stated they were a caravan carrying the supplies from their opponents. If they intercepted the caravan, they could disrupt their opponents or even use the supplies to seal their treaty with Lord Merleau. After deliberating their movements, they knew a battle awaited, and with their few troops, a handful of mercenaries, and hopefully a dragon, the scales would certainly favor them.

Lionus leaned over the map of the Silverlands sprawled out on the table, mapping their movements. He moved the wooden figure resembling House Rozea and set it firmly upon the area of the coming battle, north of Zan Rozea, near the river. *This is where it will happen. This battle will determine whether Valeciia will secure the aid she seeks from Merleau for her war.* Lionus leaned away, the scroll still in his hand.

Gervais left the chamber momentarily as he was summoned by Guido.

"Is trouble afoot?" Agustina asked, glancing at the scroll.

Burn upon receipt. I should trust Agustina, yet Valeciia wants her dead. Why? Lionus lowered his voice, "A pair of caravans is coming. The one farthest from the sea is not the envoy."

"Will it reach us before our foe's?" she asked, approaching him.

"I fear not. The battle must go on," he said, then sighed.

"Then to battle," and she pointed at the region in the map where he had placed the marker.

"You fight?" Lionus stepped back while cocking his eyebrow.

"Not in my nature. Yet I have a creature that does. You cannot come to believe that you are the only soul in Emerion with a vicious creature," she winked, nudging him.

"You are a mirror image of your sister," he said, noting her gesture. Agustina shook her head and scoffed.

Before she could reply, Gervais reentered the war room. "Your squire called for you," he said.

Let us hope Dalax is ready. It is time. And with that, Lionus dropped the scroll in the fireplace and left the pair in the war room as he wondered about Agustina's words. *What creature?*

CHAPTER 17: THE DAMNED

"What was Eleni like?" Agustina asked. The thought of Eleni was no longer like a dagger being pressed deep into his chest.

As they stood waiting in the woods for the attack to commence, she sat astride her direwolf, the beast the size of a small horse. Its fur seemed soft, yet the way it bared its teeth, he felt the beast was prepared for battle more than its rider. *Is she uneasy? Of all moments to inquire about this, why is she curious about it now?*

"Why do you wish to know this?" Lionus glanced at her, Agustina clad in leather armor, her family's rose sigil at its center. He rested his hand on the dragon's wing, leaning onto it while holding his helmet by the visor. The cure had aided Dalax's recuperation, and the speedy recovery eased Lionus' heart after his clash with Ardrien and accepting Jack's elf as his squire.

"Curiosity," she said, meeting his gaze.

They were waiting for the signal from their troops. The plan was to attack the caravan before it crossed the bridge, and then it would be their turn to join the ambush.

While they waited, he told her. Lionus spoke of his wife, recalling her wavy blond hair, the bronze skin of Emeros, the emerald eyes, and the tenacity yet gentleness the woman had. Even then, he recalled the spark of fear in her eyes when they were in the tavern. Her last words, then, the life escaping her. It still haunted him, a memory quite vivid, yet with each day that passed, the pain eased within his heart.

"You describe her as if she were a gift from the gods." There was a sweetness in her voice, even as she said this, and the way she looked at him, it was as if, through time, he could see a similar kindness to that of his wife.

"The grandest gift any man could receive," he said, pushing off his dragon. "I would do it all to protect her once more," then he paused, "but she is here no more. I must come to terms with that." *She is gone. Yet I still stand here. The past cannot be undone, and I must move on.* "Even then, she would want me to protect all those around me," Lionus said while taking Agustina's hand, "I will not allow you to be hurt by these men, by anyone."

She put her leather-gloved hand over his, sighed, then replied, "I am not her, Lionus. I will never be." There was a calmness in her words, yet her eyes seemed to hurt with each word he said.

"I know. You are you. And I will protect you for being you, Agustina. That is what matters," he squeezed her hand tenderly, "now, *we* are all that matters." He put on his helmet and removed the horn tied to his belt, handing it to her, "If danger arises, use it. I will come for you," he said while patting the direwolf. The beast, though it watched him, must have sensed his good intent and allowed him to remain near.

In the distance, a fire arrow tore into the sky, and the silence of the forest vanished. The clash of metal in the distance signaled the attack was drawing closer, and it was their time to move. *This is it. The battle has begun. May the gods watch over us, and may I watch over Agustina.*

Lionus patted her hand and clambered onto his dragon. Dalax flapped his wings, and in a couple of moments, he took to the sky. They soared above the trees, lightly grazing the beast's underbelly. His duty was to burn the bridge and the caravan's escort, for most of the guards lagged at the rear. With that, they would slip the enemy's clutches and steal the prize for which they had come.

The moment he saw the hilly clearing, he leaned in and commanded Dalax, "Drage Ignis!" and the beast hurled his flame onto their enemies.

"Dragon!" a man yelled, and those were his final words. He was incinerated, the trees around him catching fire. The bridge came alight, steam rising from the water below as it met the dragon's flame. Their enemies dispersed, rushing to the forest behind them. Across the bridge, his men overwhelmed the few guards ahead of the caravan.

As Lionus flew over them, he turned and found the clearing near the trees where he was hiding with Agustina. *She remains safe. Let us end this swiftly so we may spare needless bloodshed.* With their enemies gone, he landed, and dismounted. Agustina rushed to his side on her direwolf.

"It is done," he raised his fist. *A simple battle. How rare.* "Our men will now have the advantage, and I will escort them to Argentum."

"A plan unfolding as intended," Agustina said, though her words did little to reassure him that this was far from over. If the escort was as they claimed, it was not quite as strong to protect their caravan. *There is something amiss. There must be more.*

Then, his squire, the young elvish boy, Elrien, rushed to him. "Sir, we found the leader. Our scouts report he crossed the river ahead of the caravan with his escorts. Gervais had his commander set aside a contingent, and they stand ready to assault."

"Who is their leader?" Lionus asked, his mouth aching as he tightened his jaw. Then, Elrien described him, and with each word, Lionus' blood caught fire. It was as if the dragon itself was within him.

It cannot be. It cannot be. He is here. I will have him pay. I must capture him.

"Have you met this man?" Agustina stared at him, wide-eyed.

He took a deep breath. "Aye. We called him Darius the Damnable."

"Damnable?" they asked in unison.

"And he will be damned for stealing the ring and leaving my wife and me to die," Lionus said. "Off your horse, lad," he said, nearly yanking the elf off his mount. The boy stumbled onto the grass.

"Wait, Lionus," Agustina said, but Lionus heard nothing, his hands tightening around the reins. All he heard was revenge. All he knew was that today, Darius would see the end of his blade.

CHAPTER 18: DEATH OF THE DRAGON

Lionus rushed through the forest, past the hills with the caravan, and in the direction where Darius was. Gervais' men awaited, and as he charged, Lionus waved toward his enemies.

I will have your head, Darius. Today will be the end of you.

At full charge, the men thundered into their foes. Lionus approached from their flank, searching the men for their leader. One man, bearing a plumed helmet, stood out.

If Darius is their commander, that is him.

A group of men noticed Lionus and aimed their bows at him. His steed evaded a couple of arrows, yet two penetrated its armor. It whinnied, yet still it pressed forward in its charge. Darius' aqua plumes grew as the distance between them diminished. Sword in hand, Lionus readied himself to attack the turning horse.

You are dead.

Just as he reached him, a man appeared from the horse's flank and set his spear down.

Cursed be Malefic.

Unable to turn, Lionus clung tightly, the spear penetrating his horse. The horse collapsed beneath him, and Lionus was thrown from his mount.

Sword raised, he struck the other rider midair, and they fell to the ground, his opponent's horse rearing. Lionus groaned as his shoulder hit the ground, the man falling beside him. Twisting toward him, Lionus unsheathed his dagger. Before the man could attack, Lionus straddled the man. Without hesitation, Lionus flung his visor open.

His jaw fell agape. "Who are you?" Lionus asked, pressing the dagger to his throat.

Blood trickled from his nose, yet he laughed, crimson staining his teeth. "The last man you will see before you burn."

"Burn?" he leaned back.

How? The dragon we fought. Is it back? Where is Darius? Is he on the dragon?

Lionus punched the man, rendering him unconscious, then rose to his feet. There was a howl in the distance, pronounced, everlasting. The direwolf. Then, it was followed by a rumbling in the distance, trees snapping and cracking.

Lionus gulped.

It is the dragon. It is alive.

"Ah!" a man charged at him, sending Lionus to the ground. The man raised his sword, ready to slash him down.

Swoosh!

The man coughed, an arrowhead piercing his neck. Not far off, Agustina sat on her direwolf, bow aimed at the man. Another soldier charged, and Lionus drove his sword into the man's belly.

A third appeared.

Did we not cut off their escort?

Lionus was unable to parry him. The soldier gashed at his flank, Lionus groaning. Quickly after, the man lay on the ground, screaming. The direwolf had leapt on him. Then, in one swift motion, it tore off his head.

"We must go now," Agustina yelled, her hand outstretched.

"What happened?" Lionus touched his abdomen, wincing at the wound. It was but a gash, yet his hand was wet with blood.

"A dragon is coming. That is why Silverfang howled so."

Without hesitating, he mounted the wolf with her, Lionus and Agustina rushing away from the field.

Is Darius the dragonrider?

They reached the trees where he had hidden Dalax. Overhead, a dragon swooped over the field.

Ulrin the Unbeatable. He is back.

Ulrin set the men aflame, just where Lionus had stood moments ago. A shadow swept over them, as though the clouds had swallowed the skies, Lionus and Agustina rushing towards Dalax.

Once they reached Dalax, Lionus clambered onto the beast.

There is not much time. Ulrin will kill the men. "Go! Leave the field. I will kill the dragon!"

"I cannot abandon my father's men," she pointed toward the battlefield.

"This is no time for heroics! I cannot protect you if you are there," Lionus said, slapping the reins as Dalax began to rise.

Agustina was trembling, staring up at him while biting her lip. "The only moment we can be courageous is when we are brimming with fear. You are saving us while battling in the sky. Silverfang will care for me here," and she held onto the beast's fur, vanishing into the treeline.

I cannot allow him to find me before I find him.

Lionus began his ascent, searching the sky for the dragon, but it was nowhere to be seen. They were barely above the treeline when he heard a swoop. Glancing back, the claws were upon him.

Cursed be Malefic.

He pulled the reins, Dalax spinning, but the beast shrieked as Ulrin's claws tore at his wings.

Cursed dragon!

Lionus was certain they would hit the ground, and he held on tightly. Dalax, however, would not yield. He bit back, his teeth digging into Ulrin's belly. With his own claw, he held tightly, and their opponent roared in pain. Ulrin rose, thrice their size, and took to the skies, his rider holding onto him.

Is that Darius?

The dragons ascended, Dalax slapping him with his wings, tearing with every spike and claw in his body. As Ulrin's ascent died, Dalax released his bite and hurled a flame at him. The dragons spun out of control, spiraling down to the world below. Ulrin craned his neck and bit Dalax's own. Dalax, with shrieks tearing through the skies and fields, released, the dragons finally unhinged.

Not his neck! Will Dalax die? Is this the end of him?

Yet both creatures continued to fly, and Dalax regained his strength, chasing Ulrin beyond the cliff.

Ulrin had disappeared, and as Dalax approached the cliff, they began to ascend it.

Is Ulrin waiting for us there beyond the cliff? Lionus' grip tightened as he guided Dalax away from the cliff, rising along the opposite side. He went above it, yet Ulrin was nowhere to be found.

I must return to the battlefield. I must find Agustina.

As he fled, a swooshing sound tore through the sky again.

Ulrin is back.

He descended close to the cliff. Ulrin roared, and as Lionus glanced back frantically, the beast hurled a flame toward them. Lionus leaned forward, angling for the cliff.

"Go, Dalax, go!" His heart drummed against his chest. He cleared the cliff, the flame striking Dalax's tail. Then came the descent. The flames passed over him. He pulled the reins, slowing their pace, and Ulrin soared over them.

Once they flew past them, Lionus sighed. He slapped the reins, and his dragon attacked. Dalax clawed at Ulrin's back, then bit his neck. The rider looked back.

Darius! It is you! You treacherous bastard!

But Darius smiled even as his beast was bleeding. There was a roar, but this time, from behind him.

Cursed be Malefic. A second one?

Dalax released, and they spun away, meeting a second dragon with its rider.

It was smaller, golden. Dalax curled his wings, then flipped. The beast flew over them. Then, just as it was above, Dalax bit his neck, unfurled his wings, and latched onto it. With a single, giant claw, he ripped through the beast's underbelly, sending it screeching. It was no match for Dalax's might.

"Dalax the dragon slayer!" Lionus said.

The golden dragon roared, and Dalax bit again, snatching its neck.

Dalax clenched.

Clenched.

Clenched.

Then twisted his neck and released. The light in the golden dragon's eyes dimmed.

It plummeted, spiraling, until it hit the woods, and an explosion was heard in the distance, then a flame burst from it. Lionus raised a fist in the air and cheered.

Dalax continued to fly, wounded, and Ulrin descended upon them. Darius must have been furious, for Ulrin did not hesitate to bite them. But Ulrin missed his mortal blow, merely striking

Dalax's back. Dalax roared, then slapped his tail. He banked, spun, clawed, and struck Ulrin's underbelly. The beast shrieked and released them. Dalax, however, was weak. Dalax spiraled, and though he attempted to fly, he continued weakening, each flap unable to hold him in the air. Lionus clutched onto the reins, for he knew a dragon rider's death awaited him.

Curse you, Darius! You abandon me, then you wish to kill my dragon?

Dalax flapped, flapped, but it was to no avail. They continued to plummet. Lionus wrapped his reins around Dalax's scales, hoping it would save him.

Snap!

Snap!

Dalax's descent snapped the trees below. They were struck relentlessly, crushing all in their path. Men screamed, trees were uprooted. Lionus' hands' ached as he clenched the reins. Then, they slammed to the ground, taking the world with them.

The forest was aflame, and Ulrin flew over it, not to quell the flames, but to fan the chaos. In the distance, a man yelled, "He is going south! South to Val Rozea."

CHAPTER 19: JUSTICE

"Come aid me!" Agustina yelled, tugging at Lionus.

The world was blurry, painful, and what seemed like the weight of a thousand horses was upon him. It was as if the dragon itself was lying upon his body. Until, he realized, it was. The dragon's wing pinned his ribs, and a band of soldiers came to his aid, and they heaved it up with wooden poles to free him from beneath it. *Is Dalax dead?* But the dragon exhaled, and Lionus sighed in relief.

"All will be well," Agustina said, flinching as trees snapped and fell around the battlefield.

The forest was ablaze. *Was the battle lost? Did Ulrin decimate our men?*

The smell of iron lingered as he rose with the aid of Agustina and a soldier. They laid him in a cart, Elrien rushing to his side with Titus.

"We will heal you," Titus said while inspecting his wounds, Elrien snatching herbs from his satchel.

"Where is the dragon? Ulrin? Darius?" Lionus eyed the men, then searched the skies.

Titus and Agustina glanced at each other, and as Lionus noticed Agustina's pale face and trembling hands, he quickly remembered. He reached for her leather-gloved hands. "We must warn your father."

Agustina shook her head. "Nothing can reach them in time. I must go save them, but you are wounded," she looked down at him.

"I am well," Lionus rose, grimacing as his ribs ached from the previous weight of the dragon. "I will travel with you."

"You are in no state to travel," she helped him lie down as the men tended to him.

"I agree with the lady," Titus nodded while eyeing his wound.

Lionus shook his head, "Find me a horse, I will travel with her. See that Dalax is brought safely to Argentum."

"Sir," Titus said, but Lionus' expression turned solemn.

"Titus, do as I have said," his gaze shifted to his squire, "Elrien, you will ride with me and tend to my wounds. Titus will see to Dalax. Is that understood?"

Titus and Elrien eyed him, and when he repeated himself, they replied, "Aye, sir."

As they left, he sat upon the cart. *Will Dalax survive? Will anyone be alive when we reach Val Rozea?*

Agustina looked up at him. "Why are you doing this? I can travel safely with Silverfang."

Lionus, holding back the pain in his stomach, met her gaze, "I will not lose you, Agustina. I swore to protect you, and I will not break my word."

Will I fall short of what is required of me? Will I end up sparing her, or will I follow Valeciia's orders? I… I cannot fail Valeciia… yet I cannot kill Agustina. Why must I do this? No. Now is not the time for this. Now we must go to Val Rozea. After our quest in Argentum is finished, I will decide what must be done.

"Your duty is to Valeciia, not to me."

Lionus leaned forward, groaned, then hopped off the cart. Staring at her, he said, "That is where you could not be farther from the truth." Agustina's forehead wrinkled. "My duty is where I choose. And as of now, my duty is to you." There was a sparkle in her eye, and though he could see she was still trembling, she accepted he would join her and ceased her helpless, persuasive attempts.

They eventually arrived in Val Rozea, and it was as he feared. A sour taste lingered in his mouth - only ruins remained, the fields scorched. The tower was dilapidated and barely holding against the horizon as he stared at it. Stacks of smoke rose from where buildings once stood.

"No, he destroyed it all!" Agustina stepped back. Her eyes widened as she became pale.

A few survivors were loading bodies onto carts and taking them to their respective burials near the old house of worship. Lionus eyed the area, but he found no trace of her father nor sister. *Can it be? No. They must be here. They have to be hiding somewhere or aiding the survivors.*

Agustina found a servant and rushed toward her. "Where is Papa Guido and Rosea?"

"My lady. Rosea was escorted by the guards and arrived safely at Argentum after the fires." Then, the woman paused and gulped.

Papa Guido. Do not say it. Do not say it. He took a step forward, standing closely by Agustina.

"I fear your papa did not survive," she finally said. Lionus' heart sank, and he wrapped his arm around Agustina. "Your father was crushed by the tower. He was unable to escape the fires, I fear."

"No," Agustina raked her fingers through her hair, "this cannot be true." The servant's eyes were tearful as she looked at Agustina.

It is true. Her Papa was loved by many. Lionus drew Agustina close to his chest. *This should not have happened to her. Papa Guido did not deserve this fate. Agustina did not deserve to lose her papa this way.*

"We buried him by your mother in the house of worship," the servant said, pointing in its direction. "Forgive me, my lady. We spared no effort in trying to save him."

Agustina burst into tears, and Lionus held her close. Every sob from her made his heart ache. Though he had met Papa Guido briefly, he could see he was a kind lord. With her movements, the pain in his body was reignited, but Lionus stifled his torment, striving to be a pillar of comfort for Agustina.

"Forgive me, Agustina," Lionus said.

"No," she said as she cried onto his chest, "you are not to blame. I should have been here to save him."

"You could not have fought a dragon. You would have been gone with him," Lionus tucked her head under his chin as she let out heaving sobs. The servant had left, and as he embraced her, he traced gentle circles on her back, hoping to soothe her grief.

I cannot believe it is true. Darius truly killed him. Darius, who knew a man who was like a brother to me could become such a monster. He will pay with blood for his crimes. When this is over, I will have his head.

At first, it did not seem as if he would calm her, but he ended up easing her pain, though he could not say how long they stood there in silence before her sobs subsided. Finally, she looked up at him, her arms wrapped around his back, her eyes swollen after shedding all her tears.

"Will you accompany me to the cathedral?" Agustina asked.

Lionus nodded, and they made their way to the ruins of the burnt cathedral. Aside from the tower, this building was one of the few that remained nearly entirely untouched, though it was evident the flames had made their mark upon it, for one of its walls was half-melted.

They stood in silence as the sun set. How long they stood before it, Lionus would never come to know. While they were there, he had his arm around her, then they sat and watched in silence. Agustina stared at it, then leaned her head on Lionus' shoulder.

"I cannot understand why they would attack here, and why Papa? He was the kindest of all souls. Who would wish to hurt him?"

"Evil men trod this world. If anyone did not deserve this fate, it was him." Lionus stared at the fresh dirt before them. *Why would Darius do this? How did he know, of all places, to come down here? I will find him. This will not go unavenged. I will find him. I will kill him.* "We will find a way to rectify this."

"Darius has flown away. We cannot be certain he will be found," Agustina said, looking up at him from under her brow.

Lionus met her gaze, then took her hand in his, "Agustina, Darius *will* answer for his crime. For what he did to you and your family."

She looked at him in silence, then gulped. "And yours?"

"You all are my family," he said, cupping her cheek, "you all are my family after I returned to this world from Malefic's clutches." Agustina bit her lip, and she looked down shyly. Lionus raised her chin, their eyes locking again. "Life is a wheel. Justice always returns."

"But how may we be certain justice will prevail?" Agustina asked, reaching for his hand.

Lionus could feel the sorrow in her words, and they weighed

heavily upon his heart. She was so softspoken, yet lingering with a sadness she managed to contain after her previous sobs. He lowered his head, their brows meeting as he inhaled her flowery scent. "As long as I am with you, justice will prevail. Justice will prevail… because I am justice."

CHAPTER 20: RETURN TO ARGENTUM

When they reached Argentum, Lionus and Agustina met Rosea just outside the keep's doors. She was standing beside a guard, her eyes beaming at the sight of the group.

"Agustina! You are alive!" Rosea said as she embraced her sister.

Agustina held Rosea tightly in her arms, her eyes welling, "A similar thought crossed my mind on behalf of you!"

Rosea pulled back, "I could not leave you alone," she said, smiling weakly, but it swiftly subsided as they stared at each other. "Papa, he is…"

"I know. I know," Agustina and Rosea rejoining their tight embrace as Lionus watched. There was a moment as they wept in each other's arms, and Lionus, though he wished to join them, remained aside with Titus and Elrien, allowing the sisters their moment.

There is no sorrow greater than losing one's parent. The pain they are going through, it is indescribable.

After they finished, the group entered the keep, where Lord Merleau awaited on his throne. He nodded as his herald presented them. The hall seemed vast now that the festivities had ended and without the massive crowd within it.

"I am delighted to see you in good health," Merleau said.

"As do we, my lord," Lionus bowed lightly. "We have news from the outskirts."

"News has reached me regarding your father's estate, Lady Agustina. My heart grieves for him," Merleau placed a hand upon his chest. "He served the Silverlands faithfully to his last breath."

"I am most grateful for your kind words," she replied, holding Rosea's hand while they looked up at him.

"And your caravan and dragon have arrived," he said while turning toward Lionus. "Lady Valeciia has my full support in the coming war. That is, once we survive what lies ahead. Her opponents have launched an attack against Argentum. They are pillaging the land as we speak," Lord Merleau formed a fist as he said this.

"My lord, I will aid you in all I can. My dragon will be healed, and together we will stand to defeat our common foe," Lionus added as Merleau rose from his throne and descended the dais. *We cannot let Argentum fall. We will defend it and destroy Darius with it.*

He met Lionus, and after a brief silence, he extended his hand, "You are a man of valor and honor. I would not question it. You fought valiantly, and amidst your injuries, you escorted Agustina to her home. Valeciia is fortunate to have you amongst her knights, and Agustina by her side. I would raise my sword alongside you any day."

"You honor me, my lord," Lionus said, nodding at Merleau and shaking his hand. *Will I still be a man of honor if I kill Agustina? That is no honorable deed. To kill a woman who has been kind to me over the past several moons. I just cannot…*

"Now, a war is coming, and we must prepare our defenses. It will be a lengthy siege, and I have ordered our food stores to be transported to our warehouses. Send word to your lady, we know not what awaits us," Merleau crossed his arms over his chest.

They spoke of the siege plans, and once they were done, Merleau stated he would grant them chambers within his keep. Dalax was to be tended by Titus and the kingdom's finest healers in the keep's lower chambers.

After they spoke, Titus went to tend to Dalax while Rosea and Agustina departed to their chambers. Lionus held Elrien back, just as he received a message from a courier.

Sir Lionus,

Our caravan travelling closer to the sea was attacked. I fear all supplies were lost, and I was the sole survivor. I suspect a spy moves amongst us. Word was sent to Lady Valeciia.

Cretorian Guard

Lionus crumpled the scroll and furrowed his eyebrows.

How? How did they know? Was it Agustina? Or someone else? Who could be aware of our every move? We must lure them out. But how?

"Elrien. I have a task of utmost importance for you," he said, pointing at the elf.

"Aye, sir." And in that moment, he gave the most secretive task he could have given to an elf he barely trusted. *I cannot believe I am handing him such a task. Yet, when I am surrounded by allies I cannot trust, and enemies in every corner, he whom I trust least may prove to be my greatest ally, or my ultimate downfall.*

CHAPTER 21: FLAME DOUSER

Boom!

The castle's walls reverberated with the thunderous crash of the enemy's trebuchets. Rosea trembled, as though echoing the castle's shuddering walls, and for a moment Agustina wondered how she would calm her down.

The people of Argentum sat within the keep, holding each other and whispering to their neighbors. With the constant bombardment, sleeping would be impossible, and terror wreaked havoc through the keep as children cried and others clung to their dogs or family members for comfort.

The great hall's door opened, and a group of Cretorian Guards entered, amongst them, Lionus. He removed his crested helmet and held it against his hip, his gaze searching the hall. It was not long before his eyes met Agustina's, and her racing heart stilled as their gazes locked. He marched toward them, his armor clinking as he approached.

His face remained stern until he saw Rosea and a faint smile softened it as she looked up at him. Lionus knelt beside her, and Rosea smiled, her limbs shaking as she stood up from a chair lined against the wall.

She met him and gently grasped his arm. "Are you hurt?" She eyed the blood on his gauntlet. But Agustina did not fear for him, for his armor was intact. She closed her eyes and looked up at the heavens. *Thank the gods he is well.*

Lionus placed the helmet on the ground and looked up at the young girl, "No, Rosea. It is the blood of a fallen ally."

"And you witnessed his death?" she asked, jaw agape, her hand tightening around his forearm.

Lionus patted her arm, "There are some terrors we must face for the safety of those we care for," he said, then sat on the chair beside hers.

Our safety. That is the terror he must face for us. Rosea shuddered, as if she had recreated the image in her mind, like a canvas that could not be burnt.

Lionus gently grabbed her hand and patted his leg. "Come," he said. Agustina slid a cushion over his leg so Rosea would not feel his armor when she sat, Rosea complying and sitting gently on his lap. "What frightens you?" he asked as she sat.

Rosea remained silent as Agustina sat on the chair beside them. "What will happen if they enter the keep? Will they… Will they kill you? Will they take us?"

Lionus wrapped his arm around Rosea and pulled her close, as if she were his own child. Agustina's breath softened, a tender heat rising to her cheeks as he comforted her, Rosea resting her head upon his pauldron. "They will not take you. I will see to that. Not you, not your sister," he glanced at Agustina. Her heart skipped a beat as their gazes met. Then, Lionus looked down at Rosea, who had in her hands a wooden toy of a noblewoman in a dress.

"How can you be certain?" she asked while turning the figure in her hands.

"Because…" he paused, as if measuring his words, "because my men and I will fight to our last breath to ensure your survival."

Rosea stopped turning the figure and bit her lower lip. She turned to look up at him, "You would lose your life for us?"

Lionus glanced at Agustina. *Do not lose your life for us. You must fight for us. Live for us. We cannot lose you. Not now.* Agustina shook her head slightly, and Lionus lowered his gaze to Rosea, "A life is merely lost if it served no purpose. Protecting you and your sister *is* my purpose."

Rosea grabbed his arm, "Do you not fear death?"

Agustina's heart hitched at the question coming from her sister. *Lionus will not die. He cannot die. He is a Cretorian Knight. Cretorian Knights are meant to be invincible. They are like Valenours themselves. They are said to only fall to their own. But one of his own is out there. Darius has a dragon and a ring. What if… what if Lionus perishes? No…*

he cannot. I will not allow it. The gods will not allow it. He is a good man. Good men cannot die.

But she had seen many good men perish, and her heart ached at the thought.

"As long as the gods are by my side, there is nothing to fear," he lowered his head. "Do you wish to hear a secret?"

Rosea leaned in and whispered, "Aye," her eyes wide.

Lionus glanced around and pointed at the other children around the keep. "It is in our moments of greatest fear that we are granted the gift of courage. Rosea, as long as the gods and I are watching over you, the only fear that remains is in your heart. Quell the flame of fear that burns within you, for I will protect you until my last breath. But give me your word on this..." he said, lowering his voice.

"What?" Rosea leaned in, Agustina mirroring her, for even she did not wish to miss his words.

"Be brave for the children here, and quell the flame stirring in their hearts as well. Can you do this for me?" his eyes narrowed as he awaited her answer.

Rosea looked up at him and gulped. He smiled at her, and she nodded as she replied, "I will be brave for them. I will quell the fear in their hearts." Agustina's heart eased, Lionus pulling Rosea to his chest and caressing her hair.

Agustina leaned into him unconsciously, as if she too wished to quell the flame within her. Lionus wrapped his arm around her, Rosea tucking her head under his chin as Agustina leaned against his pauldron.

"All will be well, my child," Agustina said while caressing Rosea's cheek, her sister's soft cheek rising as she smiled at her. *May the gods calm your heart. The fear of your first siege is an unforgettable, yet haunting experience.*

Rosea whispered to her sister, "I am aware. Just as Lionus quelled my flame, I know it is you who quells the one within him."

Agustina's breath hitched at her words. *Why does she say this? Is it evident in me? Has Lionus spoken to her of me?* But she did not question it further, and Rosea lowered her head. Then she noticed Rosea resting her head against his chest, and as Agustina leaned closer toward it and her sister, she heard his heart slowing. *Clever child. You have inherited the keen hearing of our distant ancestors as well.*

She could not state how much time passed, but the three sat there for what seemed like an eternity. Rosea eventually rose and went to talk to another boy in the keep. He was trembling as she was earlier, and though the trebuchets had ceased, he was inconsolable.

Agustina looked up at Lionus, "Why are you like this?"

Lionus met her gaze, "How?"

"Of such tender heart," she glanced away.

Lionus shook his head. "Children should not suffer because of the wars of men," he paused, as if recalling the past, "there exists no feeling more terrible than feeling helpless in a place you cannot aid."

"Is that why you sent her to calm the children?" Agustina pulled away to look at him.

"It is not. I sent her away because even though she carries a flame within her, Rosea is a flame douser. She knows how to calm even the fieriest of hearts," he paused, locking eyes with Agustina, "just like her sister."

Me? Agustina fiddled with her dress. *Like our adventures? Is it because of his wife? Or does he speak because of the war? Of our moments in this journey as a whole?*

"You are my flame douser in a world riddled with children of fire." His words seemed to melt her heart. *Me? Peace? A flame douser? It is the most honeyed word a man has bestowed upon me.*

"That... that... I am at a loss for words, Lionus," she said, and he simply smiled.

"Words are the least I need from you to calm my heart, Agustina," he said, and her lips parted slightly.

Ahhh... why is Lionus like this? His words? The way he protects Rosea and me. I cannot be by his side without... no. I must calm myself. I cannot lose control here. Not now. Not in the middle of a battle. Not with him. But as she looked up at him, any sense of control vanished before she could even grasp it. Her stomach fluttered, and she grinned in a silly manner. Agustina pursed her lips. *Why now? Why like this? I cannot understand how I am swooning in this manner today. I have said things to him, but I was able to control myself. Is it because he is saying these things in return now?*

And as he looked at her, there was no way she could escape his gaze. "We all need one to calm our hearts," she finally said.

The corner of his lip curved. "Then I hope you may allow me to ease your own."

She shook her head and cocked an eyebrow in confusion. "I am calm." Lionus, however, looked down at her leg, and she noticed she had been bouncing it. *How disconcerting.* He placed his gauntleted hand over it. Though clad in Melanoriian Steel, he had a manner of placing it in the gentlest way possible.

"Do not fret," he pulled her close. Agustina was on the verge of answering, but as he held her close to his body, she stopped bouncing her leg, and her heart eased. The calmness he brought to her prevented her from replying, and in that moment she merely enjoyed the embrace.

Perhaps, just perhaps, it is not I tonight who pacifies his heart, but instead it is Lionus who is my flame douser.

CHAPTER 22: DUTY OR LOVE

Three moons had come to pass, and the siege continued. No dragons had fought, and the people of Argentum were murmuring through the streets that famish would be their downfall. With the warehouses burnt and no aid arriving, their days of survival were dwindling.

"The troops from Accreton have been delayed. Will they tear through the blockade?" Elrien asked Titus as they stood in the library.

"The gates will not hold much longer. Tomorrow evening, they will breach the city," Lionus said, Elrien and Titus looking at him. *This is a battle between them and us. We will not be able to depend on aid arriving.* "Is Dalax healed?"

"Nearly healed," Titus said, shaking his head. "He may battle, but if he takes to the skies, you must be wary of certain wounds. One strike to these wounds, and your downfall will be certain."

"Dalax or no Dalax, our lives hang by a thread. Tomorrow, we fight, or we perish," Lionus balled his fists. *Argentum will not fall, not without a fight.*

In the library, as the fire crackled, his gaze went beyond the warmth of the formidable chamber and to its balcony, where Agustina stood in a rose dress, and Rosea wore an emerald-colored one. Their time trapped in the keep had brought them closer, but doubt still poisoned his mind. He had sent Valeciia a letter inquiring about his quest to end Agustina, and Valeciia stated it had to be done, with no further explanation given. With much betrayal having occurred since his arrival in the Silverlands, he was torn: duty, or his heart.

"I will tend to him," Titus said while the pair exited the library, leaving Lionus with Agustina and Rosea.

Lionus proceeded toward the balcony, the waterfalls descending along its flanks, adding a fresh aura to the tense ambiance. In the distance, the peaceful Silver Sea was dotted by the torches in the ships from the blockade.

Rosea looked up at him as he approached, then smiled sheepishly as she played with her wooden toy. Agustina rested her hands on the parapet, gazing at the world below. Lionus joined her, and she glanced quickly at him.

"You seem uneasy," Lionus said, mirroring her as he rested his hands on the parapet. *This siege has certainly taken a toll on us all.*

"I am well," she said, then looked at Rosea. "Rosea, it is time for bed. The servant is waiting for you outside the chamber."

"I do not wish to retire to my chamber," Rosea pouted.

"Go, I will not repeat myself. The hour grows late," Agustina added, placing a hand at her back and guiding her toward the spiral staircase. Rosea looked at her, but as Agustina frowned, she complied and hurried away.

There was a hearth by the stairs, a couple of bookshelves around it. Silver stag carpets adorned the ground before it, and pillows encircled them. Though it was a library, there was a bed in a corner, with silver stag pillows, for it served as a guest chamber at times.

Agustina lay on the bed, the hearth crackling beside it as Lionus leaned against it. He admired her as she got comfortable, then turned away before she looked at him.

The stairways were met by the moon's rays as they passed through a glass dome, while galleries encircled the stairs, allowing anyone who entered to watch the library from above.

Above, the door scraped, and then it closed. They were alone, the outside of the entrance guarded by a pair of Cretorian Guards Valeciia had sent their way.

"You can sit on the bed," Agustina said as she patted it. Lionus, wearing his ruby surcoat, sat by the edge, and she rested her head on his lap. He glanced down, Agustina turning on his lap.

Lionus raked his fingers through her hair, and a light tremble escaped her. "You are not well. What ails you?"

Agustina remained silent, her cheek resting against his thigh. Then she turned to look up at him, the spark of fear in her eyes evident. "Lionus, I fear for us. The gates are nearly breached. The walls are crumbling. The people are on the verge of starving."

"I am aware," he said as he stopped caressing her hair. *I will not allow them to harm you.*

"How will we survive this? We have no aid getting through that blockade. Dalax is not entirely healed," she said.

Lionus leaned back against the wall, watching her calmly. *How could this woman be capable of treason? Of any atrocity? Look at the fear in those eyes from a simple battle.*

"We have survived this far. We will survive what is to come," he laid his hand on her stomach. Agustina grabbed his arm, as if it would save her from the perils that lay ahead. "I swore to protect you, and I will do it until I draw my last breath." *Will I? Will I forgo my duty to protect her?* He glanced at the hearth, recalling the scroll he received in Val Rosea. *The letters from Valeciia. The caravans which had been attacked. It was Agustina. If Valeciia was aware, then why did she send me those letters? Is this a test? Does she wish to see how strong I am? How loyal?* Then he looked down at her and met those calm eyes, her loving gaze. *It cannot be. Why would she betray her trust? What does she gain? It is not in her character. Agustina is brimming with love. Care. She could not. What if I do not kill her? What if the battle ends her, and I do not forgo my duty? No. I cannot allow her to die. This woman. She is… caring… lovable… dear to me.*

"Duty or love, Agustina?" Lionus asked, hoping she carried the answer to his own moral question.

"What?" she asked, her eyebrows furrowing.

"If you had to decide, which would you choose?" he avoided her gaze.

Agustina rose from the bed, then strolled to the fireplace. She stared at the flame, its light flickering against her face. It was as if she sought answers from it, but they were delayed in their arrival. Then, after a brief silence, she faced him. "Love."

Lionus rose and closed the gap between them. He looked down at her, her face half lit, half cast with shadows. "You would betray the world for love?"

Agustina raised an eyebrow, "No. There is no duty without love. If you cannot love, how can you serve? Love is the purest form of duty. If you cannot love those dearest to you, how can you ever hope to fulfill your duty?"

Cursed be Malefic. What type of sorcery is this? Lionus raked his fingers through his hair. "Never in your life would you betray the realm?"

She shook her head, "I would never. Why are you asking this? Has this siege succumbed you to madness?"

No. But you and Valeciia have.

She stepped away from the flame and made her way to the balcony, though she stopped before a bookshelf.

I could end this now. Yet, I can see it in her eyes. She cannot lie. She is not lying about this matter. Lionus walked over to her, and as he reached her, she swiveled to face him. She tilted her head and narrowed her eyes. "What is it with these peculiar inquiries? You are acting quite unlike yourself."

Lionus' heart raced. The more he looked at her, the more he spent in such close proximity, the more he questioned her. "You are like a riddle I cannot decipher."

"What is there to decipher?" she cocked an eyebrow.

"Everything." But the more he looked at her, the more answers he found. There was nothing left to decipher.

"You speak as though you do not know who I am," she placed her hands on her hips.

"I do not," he replied, his stomach hardening.

"We have travelled together and spent much time in each other's company. What more do you wish to learn of me? My favorite fabric? My deepest plot? My favorite destination in the realm? You have come to know me at my core, Lionus. What is there left to decipher? Tell me!"

He stepped toward her, "Why the realm wishes you dead?"

Her eyes widened, and she recoiled, shaking her head.

"What have you done?" Lionus added.

"I do not know why the realm wishes me dead. I have had assassination attempts, but I cannot see why there would be hatred. No misdeeds bear my name," but as she stared at him, he saw the spark of fear rekindle in her eyes. "No… no…" She took another step back as he closed in, her retreat halted by a bookshelf. Agustina gulped. "Were you sent to kill me?"

"Does it matter?" he asked, his limbs weakening with her words.

Agustina looked up at him, and she shuddered. "You were," a whimper escaped her, "why?"

"It matters little," Lionus said, his head throbbing as he unsheathed his dagger, his other hand tense.

She looked at his hand, biting her lip, her chin trembling. He reached for her arm, snatching her hidden dagger. Agustina did not react. She simply stared at him while shaking uncontrollably. Under his grip, her hand continued to tremble, clammy, and she shook her head.

"Why? Why does it matter little?" she questioned.

Her knees buckled, but he pinned her against the wall, Lionus and Agustina chest to chest. Agustina's ragged breathing beat against his neck. She stared at him. She did not attempt to fight or flee.

"Because I could not do it," Lionus narrowed his eyes. *Why must I kill her? I cannot. It is not in me. I promised to protect her. I cannot fail my duty. Yet, I cannot betray her.*

"Why? Why can you not? If it is your duty…" and then she paused. For a moment, her trembling ceased. There was a shiver in her lower lip, but the fear in her eyes vanished. She understood, and he could see it in her eyes. The question. She knew. *She knows.*

"Why can you not do it, Lionus?" she repeated, this time, her voice softer. Her words caused him to ease his grip on her arm, and he dropped his gaze shamefully. She slid from his grip, then reached for his face, raising it, their gazes locking once more. Her voice had now forgone its fear, taking on the gentle softness it had carried since they first met. While their gazes remained fixed upon each other, he knew it was she who could end him in that moment, if she had not done so by now. In a near whisper, she said, "Why can you not do it, Lionus, the Lion in the Sky?"

He remained silent. *Malefic damn you, woman. Malefic damn us. I cannot. I cannot. I am weak.* Finally, he answered, "Because the one crime you have ever committed is being a thief of my heart."

As if she was not expecting it, their breathing stopped simultaneously, and they looked at each other in silence. The world came to a halt, the battles forgotten, the crimes pardoned. Only they remained.

"Of that-" she said.

There was a thud, Lionus dropping his dagger. Then, he reached for her neck and pulled her closer.

Their lips locked, and after more than four moons, he recalled the soft lips he had found in that alley when they were escaping the streets of Argentum. Now, it was sweeter, as if imminent death, or love, or chaos, had intensified the pleasure.

Agustina slid her hand behind his neck, pulling him down. Lionus pushed her against the bookshelf, a couple of books slamming against the floor. They were undisturbed, and Lionus slid his hand up her waist and came to a halt on her neck. As their bodies crashed against each other, he grabbed her thigh, Agustina raising it as he held her firmly.

The door above groaned, and a guard called out, "Is all well, Sir Lionus?"

"Cursed guard," he mumbled as he pulled away from the kiss.

Agustina chuckled, then pursed her lips.

Of all times, do not interrupt us now. "Aye, all is well," he said. There was no reply. The footsteps receded, and the door groaned shut.

"Well, that is done," Agustina said while biting her lip.

"Yet we are not," Lionus said as he took her once more, seizing her other leg, and picking her off the ground. Agustina shrieked, books continuing to fall around them. Their lips locked once more. Agustina's legs wrapped around him, tugging him closer.

Their breathing continued to hasten, and Lionus carried her across the library. "The bed? The floor?"

"Anywhere!" she said as she pulled him closer.

This woman will be the end of me. I would risk it all for her. Damn Valeciia. Damn the war. Damn the world.

Lionus dropped her on the bed, the edge of her dress rising to her thigh. He slid his hand up her leg, Agustina shivering. He loomed over her, and she bit her lip. Their eyes locked. There was no one who could tear him away tonight. He leaned down, closing in on her. Their lips grazed, but he remained hovering over her. He shifted his gaze from one eye to the other, then to her lips. Under him, he could feel her breathing hastening, and she reached for his neck again.

Lionus resisted, then smirked. "What is the hurry?"

"That we may die tomorrow," she said, cocking her head.

"That is not our problem," he replied in a low tone. *Perhaps we may die tomorrow, yet what good will it do us tonight?* "We have the entire night to live and die. I care little for tomorrow. All I care for is tonight. For you. For us."

"Then tonight we live like a phoenix," Agustina said, Lionus impressed by her poetic ways. He pressed his body against hers as he met her lips once more. Through their locked lips, he could feel her smiling, and he could not contain himself either.

While they were immersed in their world, Agustina helped him remove his surcoat, slipping it over his head. Lionus continued sliding his hand over her thigh, the soft sensation of her skin meeting his rough hands. As he kissed her neck, her skin prickled under his touch, as though her very soul had gasped.

Agustina let out a light moan. Her low moans ignited him, and he throbbed as he closed in on her. Lionus breathed gently against her ear, Agustina biting her lip and reaching down, removing his chemise.

Lionus mimicked her movements, sliding his hand between her legs. There was warmth, and then, a sudden wetness. His fingers were moist as he slid them closer. Then he felt her, and she whimpered. He reached for her breast with his other hand, and gooseflesh spread along her skin like a quiet ripple. He played with the tenderness of her nipple, and Agustina faced him, meeting his lips once more.

"Four moons too long," she whispered, then pulled him closer, her lips hovering over his ear. A chill ran down his spine as her warm breath rushed past his ear.

His hose tensed, and he gripped her thigh. With his other hand, he removed her dress, revealing her pink nipples. Her skin was so smooth, he could not imagine letting the world lay a hand on her or injure her in any way.

He threw the dress to the ground as she removed his hose, releasing the tension building within. Agustina reached for his chest, sliding her hands down his muscular body. She did not miss a spot, her hands going over each abdominal muscle protruding over his torso until she met the tension which had been hiding under his hose. He inhaled as she grasped it, Agustina running her hand along it. As though they were at war with each other's bodies, Lionus pressed his hand over the wetness in her legs.

Agustina moaned, bit her lip, then smiled with pleasure. Lionus mirrored her movements, then leaned down, pressing kisses along her body. His lips trailed over her skin, his tongue exploring her body, circling, tasting it, until he met her nipples. Agustina slid her hand in his hair, raking her fingers through it as he continued his journey over her skin. Lionus licked her cleavage, then descended to her stomach. Lionus' fingers travelled down her sides, his nails teasing her skin, coaxing gentle peaks of pleasure, yet careful not to mar its beauty.

She moaned with each moment he went over her body. He continued to rub between her legs, and Agustina whimpered. She dug her hands in his hair and pulled him up. They were face to face, breathing rapidly. Lionus looked at her, smirking, aware of the hold she had over him. He could see she was about to beg for it, and he remained fixed upon her eyes, as if catching every ounce of desire within them. With one swift move, he went down to her collarbone and planted a kiss. Then, he made his way, alternating between kisses on each side of her neck until he reached her chin, then her lips. Agustina was quivering, and he could see she was yearning for it. She mouthed, "Please," and Lionus could not help but comply.

He lowered himself and allowed her to help him. She directed him to where she desired. He met her wetness, and she wrapped her legs around him, pulling him in. Lionus entered her wetness with ease. Agustina gasped. Lionus hardened further, and she gripped him as if she never meant to let go. He remained steady, and she drew his body closer, her hands coursing down his back.

Lionus thrust in and out, her nails digging into his skin. He arched his back, her hands tearing through his body like tiny daggers. But pain was intermixed with pleasure. With each thrust, the sensations increased. Her moans hastened, his body quickened, the nails dug deeper.

Harder. Deeper.

Harder. Deeper.

Faster.

If this was the death they spoke of, he cared little for living. His body rushed with pleasure, waves running up and down his spine. Agustina's body moved, up then down, like waves in the ocean.

Like the waves rushing through him. He held onto her hip, turning it inward, pushing deeper. She raked her fingers through his hair.

She held tightly.

Pulled him closer.

Chest to chest.

Faster. Deeper. Harder.

Every kiss sent shockwaves down his body. They moved in unison, mirroring each other, their bodies shaking as he continued his strokes. She leaned in, biting his neck. Lionus leaned closer, biting her ear, then whispered words deemed inappropriate for any nobility. But these words inspired her, for she moved faster, and so did he. Gooseflesh rose along their skin with each stroke. Their moans grew louder, their strokes harder. The fireplace could not match their flame, their bodies perspiring in a futile attempt to extinguish their desire.

But it was inevitable. Their destiny was inevitable. They were meant to meet. They were meant to live. They were meant to love each other endlessly.

Her grip tightened in his hair. He slipped his hand up her neck, creating pressure around it. There was no dousing their flame.

They went faster.

Deeper.

There was no escaping. Lionus could not hold the tension any longer. He released it all within her, and she moaned with pleasure. Both tensed, reaching ecstasy, dying, and being reborn. In that moment, they panted, looked each other in their eyes, and Lionus realized they were immortal. As long as they were together, their love was the love of the phoenix.

That night, they remained together, talking, laughing, making love, and living all the life they had withheld from each other since they met. If they were meant to die tomorrow, then Lionus knew they would die being aware they gave it all. There was no tired soul when you were ignited with the one who gave you all the life you needed.

CHAPTER 23: BRAVEBLOODS OF ARGENTUM

Lionus stared at the world below from the battlements, the grasses inexistent, now filled with the low glimmer of their opponent's armors. The rain's pitter patter hit the battlements and their armor, the men beside him shivering.

This is the moment. Our final stand. We live or die holding the line.

While he waited, he recalled the evening before he came to the battlements. Agustina had aided him in preparing for the battle ahead. They stood face to face, Agustina tightening the buckles and leather straps on his armor, straps he could have done himself. Lionus, however, watched her graceful fingers while she continued to aid him before the battle.

She took the remaining pauldron, and though heavy as they were, she carried it with an ease beyond that of squires he had seen aiding other knights before battle. Once secured, her fingers lingered a bit longer, Lionus coming to a halt as he tightened his belt around his waist.

Will this be my final moment with Eleni? Is this a tormenting farewell, or a simple respite before we are reunited after the battle?

They looked at each other, and a smile tugged at the corner of her lips, then vanished as quickly when she swiveled.

From the table behind her, she snatched his crested helmet and turned to face him. Lionus stared at it momentarily, then took it and held it against his hip. Lionus shuddered.

Will I see her after the battle? Or will I fall to another man's sword or Darius' dragon?

She went back to the table and brought a shield, a pearl-colored heater shield with a ruby rose in its center. It was freshly painted, untouched by the terrors of war.

"It does not carry your sigil, yet it is Melanoriian steel," Agustina said, handing it to him. She stared at the shield, then looked up at him, "Painted by a talented Beaumont artisan. I pray it protects you in the battle to come."

Lionus admired it as he took it from her, tracing his finger over the rose. "As much as this shield will protect me, I swear it upon my soul to protect *you* until my last breath. I will die in that battle if it means sparing you from the terrors of war."

"No," Agustina said while reaching up to cup his face, "that is a task too simple. Any man may die for me. Do not die for me… live for me."

"You do not cease to impress me," Lionus looked down at her, taking her hand in his. He raised it, planting a gentle kiss on her knuckles. "I will live for you, my lady."

Agustina smiled, then took a ruby ribbon with her family's sigil. "May I?" she asked, and he nodded. She tied it on his sword arm, her hand lingering while she looked at it.

I will be her champion, until the end of her days, or my own.

Lionus remained looking at her. It was as if she sensed it, for she turned to meet his gaze, their eyes locking in what could be their last moment together. He leaned down, Lionus and Agustina met in a soft kiss, her floral scent soothing his heart.

"I will live for you," he said as he withdrew from her, and the flowery scent dissipated.

He was met once more by the rains in the battlements, the flower scent gone, merely to be replaced with the pungent odor of piss. Beside him, a soldier in chainmail stood trembling. When Lionus looked at him, the man's gaze darted, and he stared at his feet.

To stand before any army is a brave feat, for you can be struck by sword or arrow in any instant. These men's valor, even amidst their state, proves their tenacity. A few words may be of aid.

For a moment, his arm trembled. Death could strike at any moment, but he clutched his belt. *I will live for Agustina. I will live to protect all here.* Lionus glanced along the lines while resting his hand on his sword's pommel, then stepped before the soldiers and the battlement's merlons.

Pacing between them, he said, "Any man who can stand before

arrows and fire has more valour than any dragonrider. I consider myself honored to fight alongside you men. You stand to protect the indefensible from the terrors of war. Even as we stand here, I wish you all to remember, fighting to die is much simpler than fighting to live, but fighting to live is much braver than fighting to die. All of you are men of valour, you are bravebloods."

The men remained silent, some quivering, others staring into the distance, as if the abyss called them.

Not quite inspirational?

Then, one soldier slammed his sword against his shield, "Bravebloods!"

And the remainder of the men followed in his chant, the entire battlement answering, "Bravebloods!"

A fire kindled in his heart.

There is hope.

CHAPTER 24: DOOM OF THE DRAGON

A part of the wall crumbled, and with the main gate breached, the defenders of Argentum were forced toward the interior wall. From a tower between the two walls, Lionus directed his troop's attacks. *We must hold the line and not allow them into the keep. The less time we hold, the slimmer our chances for survival.*

"Volley," he yelled, ordering a group of Muunelviel archers to fire at the main gate.

Their arrows brought down their enemies with ease. Lionus then directed a second group toward the breached wall, their arrows raining death upon their foes. As a second wave breached it, he commanded a group of swordsmen to strike their flanks. His men moved in, and then he ordered his trebuchets to fire at the incoming siege towers.

The first missed, then the second struck it right through the center. Men fell from it. They screamed as they met their demise with the world below, crushing their allies upon impact.

A soldier pointed to the sky. Before Lionus could turn, there was a screech. "Dragon!" One of the soldiers yelled.

The rains had come to a halt, and he spotted it instantly. It was spearing down, down toward his tower. Lionus stared incredulously, then reached for the crossbow on his belt. Elrien snatched his arm and pulled him down, "Are you mad? You will die."

Elrien was clad in silver-gold chainmail. As Lionus eyed the elf, he realized they would not survive. Glancing at the beast, its maw was now open, ignited with the flame of hatred.

They bolted down the stairs, the flame making its way atop the tower. Its heat emanated, the flames chasing them while they continued to rush to the inferior levels. Lionus' armor singed, and he knew if they did not make haste, he would soon become the dragon's meal within it.

There was a crash, then rocks from above tumbled down. They were hit by the debris, and Lionus slipped. He slammed against the stairs, his elbow striking hard against the stone.

Bang!

And he continued to slide. Unable to hold himself, Elrien collapsed on him, Elrien and Lionus tumbling until they hit the floor below.

Battered and bruised, Lionus rose and brought Elrien to his feet. *The gods are watching over us. How did we survive Ulrin's flame?* "We must continue!" Lionus said.

Outside the tower, the dragon had disappeared. Hordes of enemies rushed toward them, and he knew they must retreat to the higher levels. *Ulrin will return.*

Lionus raised his shield, blocked a man, then bashed him back. The man stumbled, his arms flailing. Before he could regain his balance, Lionus stabbed him in the chest. Another man bolted at him, Lionus ducking, then swinging.

Slash! He cut the man's torso, and the man met the ground.

Enemies continued to rush at Lionus, and most men around to aid him had fallen to their foes' blades. *We will be surrounded if we remain here.*

A pair charged at him simultaneously. Parry, strike! One man fell as he slashed his knee. Then the other one attacked again. Lionus kicked the man on his knee, spun, then bashed the second attacker on his back with his shield. He spun, and on the opposite side was met by Elrien's blade.

"A worthy squire!" Lionus said as they pushed away from each other.

"Watch out!" Elrien yelled, and Lionus spun to meet three men. He raised his shield, charged at the one in the center, then ducked, launching him over himself. One of them was met by Elrien's arrow, the third slashing at Lionus' pauldron. Lionus whirled and struck the man on the floor with his sword. Then, he threw a dagger at the third man, striking him straight in the neck.

Roars tore through the battlefield behind him, and he knew there was no way out. Whatever lay behind him, outnumbered them.

"Sir!" Elrien called out.

Behind him, a group of marching soldiers wearing armor similar to Lionus appeared. A fire stirred within him. The soldiers lowered their curved, rectangular shields, which seemed to hug their bodies. They set their shields side by side, locked together, nearly impenetrable. To face one was to face a Valenour itself, the embodiment of a dragon on land.

"Cretorian Guard!" Lionus yelled, and they repeated it in unison, shivers running down his spine. Lionus rushed to the side, and a group of crossbowmen appeared behind their defensive line.

"Fire!"

The charging enemies were met with bolts. Their line fell, and as they attempted to rally, Lionus rushed through his guard, the guard sent to him by Valeciia herself.

"Lord, you must reach the keep. Merleau is awaiting you!" one of the Cretorian guards said.

"Dragon!" A soldier yelled, and before they could move, a tower crumbled. Flames consumed the men in the battlements, and the soldiers around them dispersed.

The ground shook, and Lionus ran in the direction of the interior wall. As he reached it, he spotted Ulrin's snout.

Cursed be Malefic. I cannot escape this beast.

Ulrin set the men before him aflame. The fire continued toward Lionus. He leapt back, then glanced around. The flames continued to consume his surroundings.

This is it. I will not see the end of this battle. Ulrin has me trapped.

Before he could react, he hit the floor. He shook his head and glanced to the side. Beside him was the soldier in chainmail who had shoved him. The soldier who soiled himself in the battlements. "You are a brave lad."

The lad smiled, and as he stepped back, he extended a hand to him. Lionus reached for it, but a flame swept through the gate. It took all in its path. The young soldier was consumed by the fire, his screams echoing through the battlefield. Lionus scrambled back, his back slamming against the wall.

Even bravery cannot save a man from a dragon's flame.

His heart beat against his armor, the metal pieces of his savior crumbling to the ground. With his body riddled with sweat, he stared at the flames. A wing appeared. There was a crunching sound.

No! He is eating a defender from the battlements above.

Screams vanished, and the beast's wing got closer. Lionus eyed his belt.

This is the one way to survive this. The dragon horn rested there, and he snatched it. *The hour is upon us.* He raised his visor, and though breathless, he blew into it as if his life depended on it.

The horn echoed across the battlefield. Lionus' thumping heart raced with each moment. There was a screech, and he knew he had increased the dragon's fury. Ulrin's neck craned down.

Lionus lowered the horn, and he was met with the fiery eyes staring at him from the shadowy body. Lionus' chin trembled as he drew his knees to his chest.

This is how it ends. This is my doom.

CHAPTER 25: BATTLE OF BROTHERS

Ulrin's flaming eyes got closer, as if he wished to taunt his prey further. Lionus inched back, but with his back to the gate, there was nowhere for him to escape. On Ulrin's back sat Darius. Lionus' grip tightened around the horn. "Is this how you intend to kill me?"

Darius raised his visor, then looked at him, "No, brother. I seem to have failed at that. Your honor is what killed you. We could have been drowning in gold and silver ages ago."

"That is not all that matters in the world," Lionus said while reaching gradually for his dagger. Ulrin, however, noticed, and he shielded Darius from Lionus' view.

Darius smiled, "You will never know."

Lionus shook his head, "I do not need to know. We could have roamed the land together, but instead you betrayed us. You left us to die," he said, reattaching the horn to his belt and pointing at Darius.

"Eleni would not have survived," Darius said, "and you could never have seen reason with your noble antics," he shrugged.

"Reason? Silver is your reason? You have truly gone mad," Lionus' face warming as he recalled the night Darius betrayed him. "You are a greedy traitor and deserve to die by the sword! No ring, silver, or duty is worth betraying those you call family. You have no honor. I will end you!"

"I fear it is you who will meet your end. Today is your doom," then he patted Ulrin, "Drage Ignis!" he said, and the dragon's mouth ignited.

Lionus' eyes widened.

The flame came, then blew past Lionus.

What? Impossible.

Ulrin screeched, missing his target. On his wing, a giant scorpion bolt had penetrated it. Darius glanced over his shoulder, Titus aiming at Ulrin from a scorpion atop a tower.

A second screech came, this time not from Ulrin. The dragon looked up at the sky, and Darius' face paled. He slapped the reins, and Ulrin slithered away from the gate. Flapping his wings, he attempted an escape. He ascended, but Dalax scraped his wing, sending the beast crashing into a tower ahead. Dalax landed by the gate, twisting sharply.

With a grunt, Lionus staggered to his feet and swiftly made his way toward his healed beast. A shaky laugh escaped him.

Dalax, you are a true savior.

He clambered onto Dalax, his dragon laden with scars. "Volarze, Dalax, Volarze," he said without fastening himself to the saddle. He was fixed on Ulrin rising ahead, for even though Ulrin crashed against the tower, he was relentless in pursuing his escape.

Ulrin leapt to the skies, flapping for his freedom. But Dalax leapt feverishly after him. They had a battle to finish. With his rise, he blew a flame, Lionus and Dalax flying through it. Dalax's rage was evident with each screech.

The two dragons flew away from Argentum. Ulrin, though lengthier than Dalax, lacked his speed. Dalax closed in, and Lionus caught sight of Darius glancing at him.

You will not escape this time.

"Drage Ignis!" and Dalax let his flame upon their foes. When the flame struck them, Ulrin banked, then continued to rise. Dalax swooped in, baring his claws, reaching for his wing. When he was on the verge of scraping them, Ulrin twisted his neck and snapped his jaws at them.

Dalax screeched and veered sharply away, folding his wings as they twisted through the air. With that, Dalax lost altitude, falling toward the forest. Ulrin turned and chased after them. With his weight, he gained speed, Dalax unfolding his wings when the beast drew near. "We must make haste, Dalax. He is unto us!"

They flew over the forest from their last encounter, and Dalax flapped as they neared the cliffs ahead. But Ulrin bared his claws, flying over them as they were on the verge of rising. Lionus leaned forward.

I will not make it. I will not make it.

With Ulrin's claw right above them, he pulled Dalax left, Lionus and Dalax flying by the cliff, Ulrin missing them. Ulrin roared, his claws scraping the cliff.

Dalax flew away, and Lionus pulled the reins back, helping him gain elevation. Before they could find Ulrin, he vanished, and they flew toward the raging clouds.

Lightning tore through them, Lionus searching for Darius. *Where is he? Where is he?*

But he was nowhere.

Lionus flew back in the direction of Argentum, swaying, rising, and falling while he searched the clouds. But it was thick, and rain soon met him.

Not now. Not now.

With the rains, his visibility would be hindered. With Ulrin lost, this was what Lionus least needed. His hands became clammy and wet. A shiver ran down his spine when he recalled the soldier in the battlements, now Ulrin's victim.

Where is Darius? Unlike the soldier, I will not become Darius' victim. With his shoulders tight, he continued to tremble. *Where are you, Darius?*

Lightning tore through the clouds, and he started in his saddle. His knees were tight against it, and he fastened the straps to prevent himself from falling. Lionus searched the skies, but Ulrin was nowhere to be found. He glanced behind them, yet there was no beast. The skies were silent, except for the thunder tearing between each of Dalax's flaps.

Where are they? Lionus knuckles were now as pale as his face. His stomach was tight. *Where are they? They did not vanish. I know they are here.*

Then Dalax screeched. From the side of his neck, Ulrin's snout appeared. Lionus instinctively pulled to the side, Ulrin's teeth scraping Dalax's neck.

I knew they were near. They could not have vanished.

Dalax spun and clawed at the beast, but Ulrin did the same. They latched onto each other, and before Lionus could command Dalax, his dragon fought back.

Flame met flame.

Claw met claw.

Then claw met chest. Claws met wings. Flames met riders. Flames met wings. Flames ignited the skies. Both beasts spiraled through the storm. Water turned to steam, clawing turned to screeches.

Lionus had lost control. The beasts were fighting their own battle. Ulrin snapped at him. Lionus clutched for his life and leaned sideways on his saddle. Ulrin's teeth missed him by a fist.

Ulrin screeched. Dalax bit his neck. Ulrin's flames burst through the sky, Dalax's bite unforgiving.

Darius was exposed. *There you are.* Lionus pulled his crossbow and aimed it at him. He shot at Darius, but the dragons moved. Lionus missed and cursed under his breath.

The dragons continued their battle. Ulrin would not go without a fight. He bit the edge of Dalax's wing. Dalax released his bite, but Ulrin would not yield. Dalax scraped Ulrin's wing with his claw. He latched, then tore! Lightning was seen on the opposite side.

Ulrin released, spiraling. His wing slapped Dalax, and Lionus lost control as well. The dragons went past the clouds, and soon the flames of Argentum came into view. Darius attempted to straighten his beast, but the damaged wing caused his efforts to be futile.

Dalax straightened, the world continuing to spin within Lionus. As he fought to keep the contents of his stomach from rising, he held tightly to his reins. He spotted Ulrin below, the beast now straightened while continuing to lose elevation. Before he could react, Dalax speared down.

A beast untamed, a beast on a vendetta.

Darius looked over his shoulder as Dalax reached them and clawed at Ulrin's back. He latched on, then clawed at his wing again.

Swipe! Swipe! Swipe!

What was once wing was now a gaping hole. Ulrin attempted to crane back, but screeches and flame were all that escaped him. Dalax snatched Ulrin's body with his wings. Then, in one swoop, he bit his neck. Pulled back. Bit again. Scales flew. Then he bit again. The beast bled, its blood escaping into the sky.

Dalax continued unrelentingly. The treelines were approaching, and Darius evaded Dalax's rapid movements as he continued to attack Ulrin.

"Release! Release! Umitis, Dalax!" but the beast did not budge. Dalax held tight. *This damn beast will kill me.* The keep below was ever so close.

But then, Dalax unlatched, and they took to the skies. Ulrin slammed onto the keep's roof, sending stones scattering in all directions and striking down the nobles who had fled the dungeons in search of safety in the open gardens.

He created a ditch with his body, and the garden's trees along the keep's roof were unearthed. Dalax flew over, but right as they were over Ulrin, he folded his wings and landed on the beast. Dalax clawed the animal's neck, then bit forcefully.

Lionus caught sight of Darius untethering himself from the beast, and he did the same.

You will not escape!

He slid down the wing and kicked Darius off his dragon. They tumbled below. Darius fell on his back, then spun to meet Lionus. He shot a crossbow, the bolt penetrating Lionus' shoulder.

"Agh!" Lionus' body slacked back at the shot.

Darius loaded a second bolt.

Lionus glared at him. "May Malefic curse your soul!" and he ran at him. Darius shot the second bolt. Lionus evaded, and Darius began to unsheathe his sword. Lionus leapt, and with his dagger, he landed on him.

There was a groan. They were visor to visor, blood escaping from the slits. "You betrayed me. You abandoned Eleni and me. You left us to die in that forest," Lionus mumbled, spit escaping with the blood on his lips.

There was a second groan, and their bodies slackened. But they would not yield yet. A third groan escaped both. "You are not my brother," and Lionus pressed the dagger deeper into his chest.

Lionus raised Darius' visor, the man who was once like a brother to him, staring at him, blood escaping his lips. "I merely wished the best for our worlds," Lionus said. His lip curled as he watched the man's head fall back. *You will bleed and die, just as your dragon.* "This is for being a treacherous bastard."

Lionus removed the dagger, Darius struggling to breathe. *In the end, justice found you. May your suffering mirror Eleni's.* Lionus spun, Dalax rising above Ulrin, sending a victorious flame into the air. Ulrin's eyes dimmed, the flames of fury doused with his last breath as he entered the hall of dragons.

The survivors from the crowd of nobles watched from the side. Amongst them was Agustina, bow secured upon her back as she raced toward him. *It is over! We will at last have peace.*

Then, she came to a halt. She pointed behind him. "Careful!"

Lionus swiveled, and Darius placed his hand upon him. Darius was wearing the Cretorian Ring he stole from them the night Eleni died.

A flash of energy rushed through Lionus' body. "Now you die," Darius said.

Lionus' body weakened, as if life itself was escaping him, draining into Darius, giving him more life as he rose. With each moment, Darius grew stronger, Lionus losing his own vitality, his legs weakening.

"Now you will witness how every soul you love dies," Darius said, his voice becoming stronger.

He raised his crossbow. *Do not. Do not. I beg you.* But Lionus could not speak. He grew weary. He weakened with each passing moment.

Darius' crossbow rose over Lionus' shoulder. Lionus' limbs shook. In that instant, Darius shot. There was a groan. Right afterward, an arrow struck Darius' chest, and he dropped his crossbow.

Lionus fell, and so did Darius. Darius growled, snapped the arrow's shaft, and rose again. "Filthy whore," he said as he snatched his crossbow and readied a second bolt. Lionus saw Agustina from the corner of his eye. Her legs buckled, a bolt sticking from her torso.

Darius uttered a war cry. Just as he was going to shoot her, Lionus screamed, "Bastard! You deserve to burn in Arkeron!" *You will not take Agustina from me!*

Darius aimed the crossbow at Lionus and reached down for him with his ring hand. But Lionus rolled, then slashed his fingers off with his sword.

"Agh!" Darius yelled, then shot his bolt erratically.

He plopped on the ground, a second arrow striking his chest. Darius cast aside his crossbow, and as he gasped for life, Agustina arrived beside Lionus.

No. No! There was a second bolt in her chest, "Agustina!" *I cannot lose you.* Lionus dropped his sword and reached for her. He took Agustina in his arms, Agustina weak, bleeding, gasping. "No, no! Do not die. Do not die." She mumbled incoherently. "What?"

"At times, even knights need a little saving," she smiled weakly.

"You cannot die. You cannot die on me. I said I would save you. I swore. I failed Eleni. I swore to myself I would not allow this again," he said while looking at the pair of bolts on her chest.

His eyes burned, and the thought of losing her made his own heart ache. She was bleeding profusely, her azure dress tainted. Lionus glanced back at Darius, but Darius did not move.

What do I do? She cannot die. I will not allow it.

"Protect Rosea for me," she said, "live for me. Live for us," she mumbled, reaching for his hand, her touch cold.

"No, no. I will not allow you to die. I cannot live for you if I cannot live with you." *Do not die for me.* Those were her words. *But I would die for you if it meant you could live.* He looked at his ring. *Eleni saved me with it. Perhaps I can save her.*

He put his hand on her and closed his eyes. "No," she said, but he had already begun, his own body weakening. Energy rushed through it, like the lightning and thunder in the skies coursing through his body. Like if it would escape his fingertips and enter her.

"No," she repeated, her voice stronger. He would not let go. He looked at her. His cheeks became warm, tears rolling down his face. There was life in her eyes, at least more than earlier. *She is healing.* "Do not die for me, Lionus. I will not allow it." *Her strength is coming back.*

"I will not live without you," he said.

Her hand tightened around his arm. "Release me. Do not die for me, Lionus!" her fingers digging into his gauntlet.

Then, he smiled weakly, "Perhaps you will not have to." He glanced at Darius, then his severed fingers. He took his slashed fingers and removed the ring. Placing it on his other hand, he looked at Darius, somehow still alive. *I feel weak.* The world was becoming blurry.

"Lionus, let go!" but Lionus would not release her. Not in this world. Not in the next.

He reached for Darius. A second rush of energy coursed through his body. Lionus came alive. "Let go, Lionus!" *She is strong. But*

Darius is weak. He is too weak. The world started becoming a haze. Lionus turned to Agustina. "Let me go!" she pulled away. "I hate you!" But Lionus simply smiled as she tugged away, breaking their connection. He plopped back, his head slamming against the stone.

Agustina rushed to his side, still bleeding, removing his helmet. *I saved her. She healed.* Lionus could barely see her, the world a haze, all except those lovely almond eyes. Lionus smiled, "You may hate me, but I, Lionus, love you, Agustina."

"You rat bastard!" she yelled, tears escaping her eyes and landing on his lips. A blanket as shadowy as Ulrin went over him, and the last thing Lionus felt was a thump on his chest. Whether it was Agustina's blow or the wild hammering of his heart, he would never come to know.

CHAPTER 26: A VALENOUR'S MERCY

After the fall of Ulrin, the enemy's morale dwindled, and the people of Argentum overwhelmed them. The battle came to an end, and festivities were held afterward to celebrate the siege being lifted.

As the people gathered in the city's center, Lionus held onto his ribs. Titus held Lionus' steed's reins as he dismounted, and Elrien stood beside him, watching that he would not trip and hit the ground.

Lionus wore his Cretorian azure and ruby surcoat, decorated with the same sigils he wore on his armor. Elrien handed him a scroll. "As you requested, Sir Lionus."

Lionus took the partially burnt scroll with the broken Valenour seal and stowed it within his cloak. *Elrien has succeeded in his quest.*

As they entered Argentum's plaza, the scent of roasting lamb and venison drifted through the air, rich with smoke and dripping fat. As they continued, they were met with the melodies of minstrels, and the laughter caused by the jesters prancing about. From the crowd, Gervais and Baldric, the logger, were the first familiar faces to approach him.

"If it is not the Hero of Argentum. Savior of our people and our Lady Agustina," Gervais said, crossing his arms over his chest.

Lionus smiled and bowed lightly, "Thank you, Lord Gervais. I do not feel like a hero. I feel like a walking cadaver."

Gervais laughed, raising his hands in the air, a silver merchant's guild ring flashing under the sun's rays.

"You will be well recompensed for your efforts. I am certain we can find a healing concoction to aid you," he added, searching his pouch.

"Do not fret, My Lord. Titus and Elrien will be on their quest throughout the festivities today, in search of my remedy," Lionus said while tugging on his cloak. *I pray they find it swiftly.*

In the distance, the familiar laughter of Rosea and Agustina made its way through the crowd. Baldric and Gervais glanced toward it, then bowed lightly at Lionus, and Gervais added, "Much to celebrate. We will meet again, honorable Cretorian Knight."

The group bowed as the ladies joined them, and Rosea rushed to Lionus. "You are alive. The Hero of Argentum. My hero," she said, winking up at him as she embraced him, "for saving my sister," she cast a glance over her shoulder. Lionus winced at her embrace.

"Allow the knight to recover," Agustina said. Rosea released him, "He is in pain." Rosea pouted as her sister made her way toward Lionus. "Are you well?"

Lionus shrugged while grasping his wound, "I have seen better days. I have this ache in my chest. I have been wondering what may have caused it," he narrowed his eyes at her.

Agustina bit her lip and rolled her eyes, "Your rough dragon riding skills, that is for certain," she said while turning away.

"Do you believe that to be true?" Lionus leaned in, watching her closely.

"Why would I come to believe otherwise?" she asked without looking at him. "I believe you require some entertainment after all your reckless battles. It lightens the soul, perhaps relieves the ache."

"If not," Titus said, "our remedies will do." Agustina's eyes flashed as she looked at him. "Perhaps *your* remedy is quite the cure he requires." She smiled as he agreed with her.

Titus turned to Rosea, "Do you wish to join us in a potion hunt?"

"Me?" But she did not require any more convincing as she shrugged. Rosea joined Titus and Elrien, the three disappearing into the city's center in the direction of its founder's statue.

Lionus' attention was diverted elsewhere as Agustina nudged him. "What is this remedy?" he inquired while offering his arm, Agustina slipping hers through his as they joined the festivities.

"A dance. A dance cures all," she said as they found the minstrels. As if they were aware, they bowed lightly, and the tune changed to her favorite song from their night in Alzeriia.

Lionus took her hand and placed his other hand on her waist.

Her eyes brightened, and Lionus recalled their first dance, Agustina as cheerful as that night at the inn. They swayed and turned, Lionus spinning her as she let out a gleeful laugh. Then he pulled her close, Lionus and Agustina smiling, as if the world had ceased to exist around them.

"I have enjoyed our adventure in the Silverlands," Lionus said as they drew near. *Quite some time has come to pass. I have grown fond of her throughout this adventure.*

"As have I," she said, a shy smile tugging in the corner of her lip while she averted her gaze briefly.

"Do not shy from me after all this time," Lionus said, raising her chin. Their faces were now close enough that he could smell her flowery scent, that familiar flowery scent from their first dances.

"There are ladies who find it difficult not to swoon at heroes," Agustina added.

What will become of us? Our adventure is over. Our quest, finished. Lionus' stomach tightened. "Yet they met when he was but a simple man. Should they not enjoy their time as such?"

"Perhaps," she rested her head on his shoulder while they continued to dance about unhurriedly to the tune. *If time could come to a halt, I would live in this moment eternally.* He rested his cheek against her head.

They continued to dance and enjoy the day's festivities until the crowd went berserk at the sight of a giant shadow. Shrieks softened to murmurs, and excitement rippled through the crowd as children rushed forward, jumping up and down to see the grand sight.

"It is her!" they murmured.

"The Valenour woman!" another said.

"She is here! We must see her. It is truly her!"

And all rushed to see the grand dragon.

His heart halted as he pulled away, Lionus blinking rapidly. *Valeciia is here, and Agustina is alive. What will she do to her? What will she do to me? Will she end her herself, or will she simply have an assassin do the deed? Regardless, I will not allow it. I will protect Agustina with my life, if need be. I cannot let her fall victim to Valeciia.*

The crowd murmured at the sight of Valeciia. Rows of Cretorian Guards appeared by the dragon, their crested helmets rising above the crowd. Valeciia Valenour, the renowned Jewel of Emerion, made her way through them in her silk ruby dress. The guards walked alongside her, the crowd unable to join or touch her infamous snowy braid.

Upon noticing Lionus and Agustina, she joined them.

"Lionus, the Lionus in the Sky, the Hero of Argentum," Valeciia said as she approached him, raising her hand. Lionus planted a kiss upon her gloved hand, the glove matching the color of her hair.

His gaze remained fixed upon her. *Will she end me for abandoning my duty? Will she end me publicly?*

"I granted you a ring, and you brought the world to its knees for you," she said.

Lionus shook his head as he knelt before her, "For you, the Lady of Accreton. I hold no titles, except my knighthood granted by you."

Valeciia nodded as he rose, "A humble knight. A sight rarely seen in Cretorian Knights. Nevertheless, we have much to speak about. There is a task that requires completion. First, however, I must speak with Lord Merleau." Valeciia greeted Agustina, the women sharing a brief word before Valeciia departed to meet the Lord of Argentum.

After Valeciia's departure, Agustina mentioned that Gervais was to leave by the dock soon and that she wished to see him before his departure. Lionus joined her, for they did not know where their adventure might lead after today. Walking arm in arm, Lionus' arm tensed as he recalled his duty to Valeciia. *Does she expect me to fulfill my duty and end Agustina? Has she allowed me one final opportunity before she returns?* His thoughts would plague him as he reached the dock.

"Gervais, will you depart without offering a farewell?" Agustina asked as the man was talking to Baldric.

"Agustina, I could never depart without seeing you first," he said, coming to her side and planting a kiss on her hand. Then, he embraced her lightly and looked at Lionus. "I trust the two of you are enjoying your final festivities."

"A most cherished respite after our arduous adventures," she said, returning to interlock her arm with Lionus, squeezing it gently and resting her head on his shoulder.

Gervais chuckled, "I have come to admire the two of you. Quite the survivors of this perilous world."

"As are you and Baldric," Lionus added, nodding at the men.

Quite the survivors. "Emerion *is* a perilous world, but with the right friends, survival is possible, is it not?"

Baldric nodded, and Gervais replied, "I could not have said it better, friends," and his gaze shifted toward Elrien as he joined them. "The party merely increases. I am certain many adventures await you!"

Lionus looked at Elrien. *Will they? Will Elrien be around for quite some time? He has proven himself. Perhaps he is a Muunelviel worthy of our company.* "Aye. What is to come is uncertain," Lionus said, "but if I am certain of one thing, it is that we did not wish to see the two of you depart without our farewell and one last toast," he pointed to the servant standing by a crate, "does your servant have any wine for our farewell?"

Gervais' eyebrows furrowed, but without a word, he nodded and turned to his servant. "Lad, fetch us goblets and wine." The lad did as he was ordered, and he soon returned with a bottle and poured it into everyone's goblet.

"A toast," Lionus said while raising his goblet as the others joined him. "To Emerion, to a perilous world, and to survival amongst friends!"

Gervais paused. Lionus continued to look at him, smiling and raising his goblet in his direction. "To friends," the group said in disunion.

They raised their goblets, and as Gervais and Baldric took their first sip, Lionus came to a halt right at his lips, his gaze flicking to Agustina. "Is this wine adequate for you?" Lionus asked her as Gervais and Baldric gulped. Elrien eyed them, then lowered his goblet without taking a sip.

She stopped and looked at him, cocking an eyebrow. "Why would it not be?"

"It is not of the best quality for a lady like yourself," Lionus said. *She does not deserve this drink. She is not the equal of Gervais and Baldric.*

Agustina cocked an eyebrow and glanced at Elrien, her expression turning into a frown. "Are you being a jester now, Lionus? Amidst a toast?"

"How could I? A lady as yourself deserves the best," then Lionus turned to Gervais, placing his hand on his pommel, "does she not?"

Gervais and Baldric had drunk half their wine when they brought it down. Gervais frowned, "This is quite decent wine. We carry the best with us wherever we go," he said, his silver guild ring clinking against his goblet.

Lionus stood silent, then nodded. "Ah, perhaps you are not mistaken. I was merely confused. I had come to believe Agustina had tasted this wine before."

"Where would I have tasted it?" she held the goblet, Lionus looking at her.

"Why, Alzeriia, most certainly," Lionus smirked. Gervais coughed. Lionus turned to him, "Is something amiss, my lord?"

"A-Alzeriia, you said?"

"Why yes? Is this not the fine wine you brought for us there?" Lionus glanced at Agustina, then grabbed her goblet. He spilled it onto the planks, Elrien mimicking his movements. "Oh… aye… it was. The one meant for Agustina, which our friend Wilken had."

"You are mistaken," Baldric shook his head, "we brought no wine."

"Hm," Lionus turned to Gervais, "perhaps I am. Perhaps I am mistaken about disappearing caravans. Vanishing scrolls. Burning of cities. Or simply mistaken of wine? Am I mistaken, *Lord* Gervais?"

"What madness are you speaking of?" Agustina grabbed Lionus' arm. "Are you deep in your cups?"

"What madness am I speaking of, *Gervais?*" Lionus tilted his head slightly, his gaze fixed upon him.

"You are confused. Too many cups for a knight in one day," he chuckled nervously.

"It may be so," then Lionus reached for the scroll in his cloak, slightly burnt at the edges. "Or perhaps this scroll found by Elrien in your chest, with the seal from Valeciia Valenour, might rekindle your memory."

"You are mad!" he stepped forward, the veins on his temples snaking along it.

Lionus pointed at him, "This man is a scoundrel. A traitor. He learned our secrets, plotted within our courts, made us lose our caravans. In Alzeriia he attempted to kill you. If not for our dance, it would have been you dead, not Wilken. Can you not see the fright in his eyes? I would not be surprised if he planned your father's death."

"It is madness! He is a friend!" Agustina yelled, stepping away from Lionus.

"It may be so. If I am mistaken, then there is nothing for him to fret about. It is the same wine they brought," Lionus stared at Gervais. But there was an evident fear in his eyes, and Lionus was certain it was him. *Gervais, you will pay for betraying us, for your attempt on Agustina.*

He remained silent, then shook his head, "You are mad, lad! I will have justice served for your attempt on us."

"Not attempt," he pointed at Baldric. He had begun to choke and fell on his knees.

"Kill them!" Gervais yelled at his men, his nostrils flaring as he looked at his friend falling to the ground.

They unsheathed their swords and rushed toward Lionus. Agustina took a step back, and Lionus shielded her, Elrien stepping beside him, sword drawn. *If I must fight them, this will be a painful battle with my lingering wounds.*

Then, as Gervais continued to yell madly at his men, the clinking of armor and thunderous footsteps reverberated through the air. Behind the trio, Valeciia's Cretorian Guard arrived.

At the sight of them, Gervais' men took a step back. Her guards formed two rows, and the Valenour woman appeared. Valeciia stood flanked by her men, traversing their lines until she reached Gervais. She stared at him in silence.

"Ah, Gervais," she finally said.

"You damned whore!" Gervais yelled at her, then coughed. He clutched his neck.

"Did the cat catch your tongue, or does the wine not suit your noble taste?" Valeciia said with her arms crossed behind her back. Gervais reached for her, but fell to his knees, choking, gasping for air. He attempted to curse her, but no words escaped him.

"When you betray the Valenours, you burn, or you drown," she said while taking a step forward. Baldric lay motionless beside Gervais, poison having taken the best of him. Gervais dropped on his side, his body weak and stiffening. He panted, breathing slowly while he blinked rapidly, stuttering as she continued to stare at him. Agustina covered her lips, her eyes wide at the scene unfolding before her.

Valeciia crouched, grabbed his hand delicately, and removed the ring. She eyed him for a moment, as if watching the fear in his eyes. Then, she rose and placed a foot on his belly, "Today I will be merciful. Today, you can drown in your poison," and Valeciia pushed him off the dock, leaving him to fend with his paralyzed body, his body sinking into the Silver Sea.

CHAPTER 27: THE VALENOUR'S MARK

Lionus and Agustina stood above the city of Argentum, in the high gardens where the dragons had crashed before the siege's end. They watched the city below, the people dotting the landscape through the city streets, the festivities continuing even as they had retired to the keep. The cascades along the walls could be heard, the sun no longer glistening upon them, for its final rays were trapped by the mountains in the west, like little fingers clinging to life over their peaks.

"Do you truly believe they killed my father?" Agustina asked while Lionus sat on the bench beside her.

"Elrien found some scrolls regarding the estate. I fear he had to rush before he could finish reading them. It seems, however, your family stood in the way of something he desired," Lionus said, taking her hand gently in his bruised palm. *Why would they do this? I cannot believe we never found the truth behind their assassination.*

"Do you believe we may still retrieve his chest?" Agustina asked, placing her other hand over his, drawing circles atop it. Her touch had a way of slowing his heartbeat in a way he could never come to explain.

"Valeciia had someone search his chambers before Merleau entered it. It appears he was not alone. The person who was with him must have taken his belongings or burnt what was left of his scrolls." *I wish I knew. I wish I knew.*

"Hm," Agustina looked down. "It seems we may never learn the reason behind it. Was it for him, or was it for a grander scheme?"

"Whatever the reason may be, I will protect you from any peril which may come your way," Lionus squeezed her hand. *I will not allow anyone to cause you harm.*

Agustina met his gaze. There was a pause, and the muscles in her neck tensed as she gulped. "I fear I will not be returning to Accreton. Not now, at least."

Lionus' stomach tightened, balling his hand into a fist. She must have sensed it, for she stopped her tender touch upon his hand. "I cannot protect you if you stay."

Agustina smiled, "Lionus, you have the kindest heart. I must stay in Argentum to rebuild my home and care for my sister. Even when enemies lurk everywhere, I fear Accreton will merely endanger my life further. Any person with close relations to the Valenours is in peril. Even now, war has made its way across the land to Argentum, where we least expected it," she said, then pursed her lips. A sigh escaped her, and Lionus cupped her cheek. She leaned into his touch, grasping his forearm.

I am close to the Valenours. My presence endangers her. I cannot bring more chaos into her life. "If I had known that having you beside me on this quest would have endangered you, I would have continued alone."

Agustina's eyes widened while she shook her head. She lowered his hand. "You could not have known. Besides, it was not you who brought me into this perilous world. I am what my decisions make me. I chose to serve you *and* Valeciia in this journey."

She is not mistaken. Serving the Valenours comes with its perils. The war, the mere idea of being close to them… it puts anyone's life at risk. He inched closer, "And that is why now I will serve you and watch for your safety, regardless of what is to come."

Agustina blushed as she looked away, "Your place is not by my side."

"My place is where I choose it to be," he balled his fist. *I cannot let her go, not now. Not after all we have lived together.*

"You have a duty," Agustina bit her lip.

"My word and duty are tied to the realm, yet I am torn by the duty my heart has for you," he said, a tightness in his chest. Lionus and Agustina closed the gap between them.

Agustina remained silent, looking at her lap. Her shoulders rose and fell, though a sigh never came. "Lionus, why do you make my life difficult?" she tapped her foot. Agustina stopped when he drew away. "Yet each moment worth living?"

He could not find the words for her, but he knew it all to be the same. *I do not wish to be away from you.*

She continued, "Though our journey has been short, you have become family. You will forever *be* family. What you have done for Rosea, for me, it is beyond words." She paused. "What will become of us?"

Before Lionus could answer, she drew away. Her gaze was fixed behind him, and he swiveled to follow it. Valeciia had arrived in the gardens, ever so quietly, like a mouse in the night. In the distance, by a pair of trees, a pair of Cretorian Guards stood keeping watch. *Have they come to kill Agustina? To kill me for not fulfilling my duty? I will not allow it.* Lionus' heart raced, and his legs tensed.

"I imagined the two of you would seek solace far from the festivities," Valeciia said, her arms crossed behind her back. "I do not wish to interrupt, yet I must have a word with my Cretorian Knight before I take my leave."

Agustina nodded and gave her warm regards to Valeciia as she departed the gardens. "You know where to find me once you are done," Agustina said to Lionus.

Valeciia watched her leave, then raised her dress and sat beside Lionus. "I see you have become fond of her," she said.

"She has managed to save my life," Lionus said while looking at her, "and rekindled a spark I believed to have lost when you found me."

A spark I will not allow Valeciia to take. I will not debate it for a moment. I will protect Agustina, even if it means trading my life for hers.

"There seems to be much life in your eyes now, even when you managed to escape death numerous times," Valeciia folded her hands on her lap.

Is she waiting for me to tell her? How do I tell her? I cannot kill Agustina. It is not within me. I cannot. I will not. "I must speak to you regarding my task," he finally said. Valeciia's azure eyes remained fixed upon him. Icy, calculating. *Will this lead me to a fate similar to Gervais?* "I fear I cannot come to fulfill my task."

Valeciia remained silent. She looked at his eyes, then her gaze moved unhurriedly. It was as if she were searching for something, and he could not help but tense. *Will one of her Cretorian Guards gut me? Will this be it?* His throat was dry, and though he wanted to take a gulp, he could not bring himself to do it.

"Why is this?" There was not a twitch in her expression.

"Though it is my duty, I cannot betray the woman who has aided me all this time. I find no reason to end her," Lionus answered, matching her expression.

Valeciia remained silent. Only the distant sounds of the festivities could be heard. Even then, the festivities' cries were deafened with each thump of his heart. "You love her," she said.

His heart hitched.

Valeciia smiled, a soft smile, a caring gaze in her semblance he would have never imagined to see. "I recognize those eyes wherever I find them. I know what it is to love and be loved, even when you are told by the world you must not," her gaze drifted momentarily, as if she was recalling an earlier memory, one so far gone, you could barely fetch it, yet so near, you could still feel it deep within your heart.

"You do?" But she did not answer. *How could a woman so calculating, so deep in her war, who sent me to kill her friend, have been in love and felt love before? Is this the different side of her Agustina mentioned once?*

"I am very fond of Agustina. I would not have wished for you to gut her," Valeciia said, her solemn expression returning.

"Then why grant me such a task?" he cocked an eyebrow.

"A test. Cretorian Knights, there are nine. Yet all carry distinct personalities, and with them, morals. There must be balance amongst them, for war requires men of good and duty. Its horrors, nevertheless, require a darker side of man, which, at times, is necessary. I was certain you would not be the latter."

"And risk, Agustina?" *How was she certain I would not kill her? That I would not follow through on her request?*

Valeciia smiled knowingly, "I knew you would not come to do it," then tapped his arm, "perhaps you do not recall, but many moons ago, you saved me," she looked into the distant mountains, toward Accreton, as if recalling the exact moment it happened. *I saved her? When?* She met his gaze once more, "Perhaps you have been a knight at heart for so long, you can barely recall the numerous moments you have helped others," she nodded approvingly. "Even if the slightest chance of failure existed, I had

Titus watching over my friend Agustina." Then she paused briefly, taking a more solemn tone, "Men can be unpredictable in the most pressured circumstances, yet you have proven once more, love can be stronger than duty. If you cannot protect those you love, how can I trust you will be a man of duty to me?" Valeciia asked.

Valenours, wise but curious. Are they all this dark? Is there good in them? "Love is stronger than duty," he finally replied.

"And love must not be lost in a world so ephemerous," she glanced in the direction Agustina had left.

"It is a tragic story, Agustina and I. It is not yet our time to be together," he glanced in the direction she had left. He sighed, an emptiness settling within him, as though her departure had taken something he could not name.

"Yet it will be," Valeciia said, patting his thigh. His leg tensed. *Who is this Valeciia?* For a woman who demonstrated such strength, there was a way he could not help but wonder about her much softer side. "The gods work in ways we cannot truly grasp, but in the end, all things fulfill their purpose in due season."

"I believe so. I believe so," Lionus said, glancing down at her hands as she folded them back on her lap.

"A war awaits us. Before we leave, you must say your farewells," she fell silent for a moment, as if recalling another memory. "We know not when our final day will come, particularly when you live with fire."

Lionus nodded, realizing the war he had just stepped into. A sinking feeling gripped his stomach. *Have I chosen wisely?* As he was about to rise, she said, "Lionus. My ring? The one you acquired from your defeated rider."

Lionus recalled the ring he had captured from Darius. As he returned it to her, he asked, "These rings. They all have powers?"

"Magic embedded in them by our blood, that of my mother. These two are particular. The one you have heals, yet it drains your life," then she looked at the one in her hand, and she lowered her voice. "This one, it replenishes its user, yet it drains the victim it touches. It is a treacherous one," she said while sliding the dragon ring on her finger.

That is how I was able to save Agustina without perishing like Eleni. If not for both rings, one of us would have certainly perished. "I never imagined their power could be compounded."

"You played the gods, and you survived," Valeciia said, but she shook her head. "I am glad you saved Agustina, yet it is a grievous game one should never play. With these rings comes immense responsibility." Valeciia rose from the bench, Lionus standing beside her. "Now that you have fulfilled your duty to me, you are officially a true Cretorian Knight. What mark will you bear?"

"Mark?" *What is she speaking of? Will she have me branded like an animal?*

"Aye," she lifted her cloak, revealing her inked markings. "All Cretorians are eternally marked on their arm. They are the only ones allowed to be marked besides the Melanoriians. They tend to carry the mark of their house. Do you have a house?"

I do not. What mark will I bear? The words echoed through his mind: *Though our journey has been short, you have become family. You will forever be family.*

In that brief moment, he knew what his mark would be. Lionus looked up at Valeciia, "I will bear the thorned rose."

"The thorned rose," she nodded approvingly, smiling softly. "The protector."

CHAPTER 28: THE LAST DANCE

Lionus entered Agustina's chamber, Agustina standing by the fireplace. He made his way to her, the flames' glow reflecting upon her skin as he got closer. She pivoted toward him, Agustina frowning as he reached her.

"What has Valeciia said? Will she end me for you not completing the deed yourself?" Agustina asked, her eyes wide while she awaited an answer.

The hairs on his nape rose. Lionus closed in on her. "No. She will not. I have spoken with her." *I would never allow it.*

Agustina seized his forearm, "Did she say why she wished me dead? I could not come to make any sense of it."

"It was a test," he said calmly.

"A test?" she squeezed his arm, "what test?"

"A test of my loyalty. To see if she could trust me as her Cretorian Knight," Lionus said while shaking his head.

"Has she gone mad?" Agustina raked her fingers through her hair as she paced before the fireplace.

Perhaps the Valenours are all mad. Perhaps we are all mad. Perhaps madness is a simple cycle of the world. "She would not have allowed me to kill you, even if I failed."

"How can you be certain?" she asked, stopping and staring at the fireplace while cupping her mouth.

Can we ever be certain of anything? "She said she knew I would never come to do it. She says I saved her life once and knew I did not have it in me to slay you. Even then, had I failed, she said Titus would have protected you."

"Titus?" she met his gaze, cocking an eyebrow. "She is mad! I believed her to be my friend, and here she is, ordering you to end me. How can I trust her? How can I know I will be safe?" She had turned pale and was glancing about as her legs weakened, causing her to lose her footing.

But Lionus took her hand and tugged her toward him, embracing her. "I can see you fear for it all, but do not fret, Agustina, you are safe. I will keep you safe, as I have previously said." *No one will harm you. I will make certain of it. Not any man, dragon, or Valenour.*

They remained silent, and he admired her, placing a hand on her hip and keeping her close. Lionus and Agustina remained in an embrace until her body eased against his. "I will make certain you are at peace. You will be safe with me," he said, and she nodded while resting her cheek against his body.

Time passed, and Lionus remained in a pensive state. *What if this is our last time together? What if we never meet again?* Lionus gazed at her. There was a way in which she looked at him that he could not understand. *What have I done to deserve this?* She seemed fond of him since they met, but now, now there was a softness in her gaze that could strip even the toughest knights of their armor.

Lionus reached for her chin, tilted her head upwards, then leaned in closer until their lips met. This time, they lingered, as if savoring the last moment their lips would touch. With his thumb, he caressed her cheek, then slid his hand to the side of her neck as he pulled her closer. He took her in, as if each moment in their kiss would extend his life, as if each kiss would bring the sands of time to a halt.

Finally, he pulled away, their gazes locked. In the distance, there was a tune making its way past the balcony's curtains. It was a tune as old as the Valenours. He took her hand, leading her toward the balcony. "Come."

As they reached the balcony, the wind welcomed them. Lionus placed a hand on her waist, drawing her close once more, while his other hand found hers, as though inviting her into a dance. He looked down at her, "I am certain you know this song. I would wager it is your favorite."

"A wager well won," she smiled. "The tune the diamond dragon rider dedicated to the princess before the Fall of Valenoriia."

"Some would dare say it is the grandest love story of all time," Lionus winked.

"Any cultured creature would certainly know this to be true," Agustina winked back.

As he nodded, she placed her head against his chest, and they continued dancing. They spoke of The Fall of Valenoriia, of why Agustina believed it was the greatest romance of all time, and why it was such a turning point in the history of the realm.

"That was true love," Agustina said, looking up at him. "He fought until the end for her, regardless of what it cost. His love for her was unwavering. He did all he could to protect her and make certain she was loved." She stopped dancing, then pulled back, her gaze still fixed upon him, "I mean, he did what was believed to be impossible. Thanks to her, he tamed the untameable."

There was such a happiness in her eyes when she spoke of the things that moved her. It was like placing the entire night sky within them and watching it light up the world. *How can one leave a beacon of light? How can it be done?* "What will become of us?" Lionus finally asked in a low tone.

Agustina's smile faded, and she bit her lip, looking down. She shook her head, then met his gaze, "I wish I were a seer," she said while resting her cheek against his chest. Lionus wrapped his arm around her, and they continued to sway side to side. "Yet, I am slightly glad I am not. Is that not what life is about? Enjoying the journey? The discovery?"

"Perhaps. I believe it is more about the company," Lionus said as she tilted her head upwards. He tucked a strand of her hair behind her ear.

Agustina pursed her lips, then tore her gaze away. She remained silent momentarily. "Do you believe in fate?"

"I like to believe I have my own choices. Yet, I enjoy believing that everything in our life occurs for a particular reason as well," Lionus said. *Perhaps we are destined for a certain life, but the gods must have granted us a particular moment to make our own choices. If not, then what life is this?*

"I am glad you believe so," she said, her eyes shining.

"It is the simplest, logical ideal. Why would the gods bring us together to separate us?" Lionus asked. *It is nonsensical.*

Agustina remained silent, and her chest heaved as she let out a near-inaudible sigh. "A sick jest?" she attempted to chuckle, but he had come to learn she was simply making light of the situation.

Lionus pulled her away, then cupped her cheek, drawing her gaze to his. "I would never believe they would unite us as a simple jest. If they did, I would meet the gods, and make their palaces tremble for ever daring to fiddle with our hearts."

Agustina's eyes widened as she pursed her lips. "You sound like him."

Lionus cocked an eyebrow, "Who?"

"The princess' lover from the Fall of Valenoriia. The Talon King."

Lionus' jaw dropped, "Are you calling me mad?"

"Mad in love," she said. Then, as if realizing what she had said, she tore her gaze away. A light tremble escaped her, but Lionus drew her closer, and their gazes locked once more.

"I would take that madness over any other," he said, his heart racing, Agustina blushing.

Agustina pulled away. "I am pleased you believe so," and she walked away. Beside the fireplace, he heard a click as she opened a chest and retrieved a clinking object from it. She returned to him and revealed within her hand a rose necklace.

"If you will succumb to madness like The Talon King, you may very well carry a token from your lady to resemble him," she said.

Lionus reached for it, but Agustina snapped her hand closed. Without a word, he understood. *A token from my lady. It must be received appropriately.* Lionus lowered his head, and she placed the necklace over it, the rose pendant resting gently on his chest. "May I succumb to madness to protect my lady if peril ever finds her."

Agustina nodded, "May the gods protect you as they protected the King of Valenoriia during his war."

That night, they spent it together, laughing, talking of journeys past and of feasts. Together, they shared their last moments by the fireplace, for they knew not if fate would bring them together once more.

As morning came, Lionus was by the courtyard with Titus and

Elrien, Dalax sitting behind them. The pair were preparing their horses to depart for Accreton, for their time in Argentum had finally come to an end.

"I will meet you in Accreton. I have one more matter to tend to," Lionus said. *This is my last moment with Agustina. I must do one final thing with her before I depart.* The men bowed, and with their horses saddled, they mounted and departed from the courtyard.

Lionus was met by Agustina, her body lightly hugged by a rose-red dress. As she reached him, she glanced up at his dragon. "He has healed well."

"Aye. Titus and Elrien have been kind to him," he patted the dragon's scales.

They stood there, looking at each other in silence, Agustina with her arms crossed before her. "This is it," she finally said.

"It seems so," Lionus replied, his heart sinking. Then, he smiled, "There is, however, one matter we have not tended to."

Agustina's eyebrows furrowed. "What matter is that?"

"One last flight," Lionus said. *As it began, it should end. One final gift for her before my departure.* "There is something you must see."

And Agustina did not hesitate. There was a light hop as she got closer to Dalax's side, her excitement evident with each step. Lionus aided her to mount.

With her mounted on the saddle before him, Lionus wrapped his arms around her, protecting her with the reins. "Volarze, Dalax!"

Dalax flapped his wings and the men around the courtyard rushed away. It was not long before Dalax took to the skies, flying directly over the forests west of Argentum as Lionus made him bank to his right.

"Where are we going?" Agustina asked as the breeze lifted her hair, the familiar flowery smell striking Lionus as he leaned into her.

Dalax ascended, past the clouds, as they circled their way to Argentum. Lionus peeked over her shoulder. "They say Argentum looks like a dragon from the sky. Today, we will see if this is mere hearsay." Agustina gasped.

As they returned to Argentum, Lionus said, "Hold on tight!" and he eased on the reins. Dalax folded his wings, spun, then speared down. Agustina held onto the saddle while letting out a shriek, the dragon roaring with her.

Staring down at the city below, it indeed seemed to resemble a dragon. The keep's walls with their cascades resembled the dragon's wings. The keep itself was the body, and the stairs leading to it were like a dragon's tail. On the opposite side, a giant tower extended with a bridge from the keep, and if looked upon carefully, it seemed to form the dragon's head.

"Not legend," Agustina said, glancing back.

Lionus smiled, pulled the reins, and leveled the dragon, the beast flying past the tower, the guards taking cover as if they feared falling off with the wind gust caused by the beast.

Lionus hooted, then grinned. They ascended once more, high past the clouds, the cities, castles, and towns vanishing. He flew with Agustina over them, and her body relaxed against his, Agustina's head resting against his shoulder while his arms continued to encircle her. It was then that Lionus knew there was nothing in life that could compare to having your lover within your arms.

And with that, they enjoyed their last ride together before Lionus returned to Accreton. Yet, in that instance, the sands of time seemed to halt, for they knew that in life, neither the future nor the past mattered, but rather, it was the simple moments of the present that gave life to their very being.

Map of the Silverlands

ABOUT THE AUTHOR

J.C. Rose's passion for writing ignited at the age of 12 with his first short story, and since then, he has eagerly whisked anyone willing to embark on adventures beyond this realm. Currently, a nomad navigating the eastern coast of the USA for graduate studies, he is accompanied by his Siberian Husky, Akira. When not immersed in academia, J.C. can be found engaging in sports or other athletic pursuits, exploring new locales with friends in his current state of residence, crafting novels or poems, and unwinding in bookstores and cafes. You can follow J.C. Rose and stay updated with his new releases on Instagram: jcrose_official and Facebook: J.C. Rose.

Check World Anvil: J.C. Rose for Maps, Wiki, and Family Trees

www.ingramcontent.com/pod-product-compliance
Lightning Source LLC
LaVergne TN
LVHW090609110826
845146LV00001B/320

* 9 7 9 8 9 9 3 9 8 8 1 1 5 *